The broken pieces remind me of Grammy's puzzles. Although I've never understood the point of puzzles—and why you'd sit for hours trying to put a picture that's been broken into hundreds of pieces back together. Plus, when you have the cover, you know exactly what you'll get in the end.

I guess I am sort of like a pile of puzzle pieces that have been dumped on the floor. But I can't put the pieces together because I don't know what the picture on the box is. I don't know who I am—or how many pieces I might be missing. And since Aimee shone a light on something that was in front of me all this time, it makes me wonder what else I'm not seeing.

Looking at the broken pieces, I feel broken, too.

ALSO BY LYNDA MULLALY HUNT

One for the Murphys

Fish in a Tree

SHOUTING
AT THE
RAIN

Lynda Mullaly Hunt

PUFFIN BOOKS

PUFFIN BOOKS
An imprint of Penguin Random House LLC, New York

First published in the United States of America by Nancy Paulsen Books, 2019
Published by Puffin Books, an imprint of Penguin Random House LLC, 2020

Visit us online at penguinrandomhouse.com

THE LIBRARY OF CONGRESS HAS CATALOGED THE NANCY PAULSEN BOOKS EDITION AS FOLLOWS:
Names: Hunt, Lynda Mullaly, author.
Title: Shouting at the rain / Lynda Mullaly Hunt.
Description: New York: Nancy Paulsen Books, 2019.
Summary: Delsie loves tracking the weather, living with her grandmother,
and the support of friends and neighbors, but misses having a "regular family,"
especially after her best friend outgrows her.
Identifiers: LCCN 2018051566 | ISBN 9780399175152 (hardback) |
ISBN 9780698196940 (ebook)
Subjects: | CYAC: Grandmothers—Fiction. | Family life—Massachusetts—Cape Cod—
Fiction. | Friendship—Fiction. | Neighborliness—Fiction. | Weather—Fiction. | Cape
Cod (Mass.)—Fiction. | BISAC: JUVENILE FICTION / Family / Parents. | JUVENILE
FICTION / Social Issues / Drugs, Alcohol, Substance Abuse. | JUVENILE FICTION /
Social Issues / Emotions & Feelings.
Classification: LCC PZ7.H9159 Sho 2019 | DDC [Fic]—dc23
LC record available at https://lccn.loc.gov/2018051566

Puffin Books ISBN 9780147516770

Printed in the United States of America

Design by Marikka Tamura
Text set in Century MT Std

1 3 5 7 9 10 8 6 4 2

For Nancy Paulsen
who has strong shoulders

Greg, Kim, Kyle, and Dave
Long ago, I dreamed of having my own family;
you make me happier than I'd ever dreamed

Contents

Chapter 1

UNTIL NOW

There are two kinds of people. People who like surprises and people who don't.

I don't.

And yet here is Aimee Polloch, my friend since first grade, marching through our front door as loud as a summer crow. "Delsie. I have the *best* surprise."

Uh-oh.

"*So,*" she begins, "you know that Michael and I tried out for the summer production at the Cape Playhouse, right?"

"Yeah?" I ask.

"Michael got a great part, but I . . . *I* got the lead! The *lead!* Can you *believe* it?" She goes dead serious. "Wait. *Autographs.* Do you think people will actually ask for them?"

"I think we'll have to get a red carpet leading up to your front door."

"This is *no* joke." She leans forward a bit. "Do you *know* how many famous people started acting at the playhouse?"

"I think you've mentioned it," I say, smiling.

After one giant step, she stands right in front of me. "I *really* need your help, though!"

"*My* help? Why would you need *my* help? You know I'd rather hang glide in a hailstorm than be in a play."

She shakes her head. "I don't need you *in* the play, Delsie. I just need you to help me with my part. The play is *Annie*," she says, wide-eyed.

"The hard-knock-life *Annie*? The movie we watched?"

She rolls her eyes. "It was a play *long* before it was a movie."

"Whatever, Aims. You know theater isn't my thing."

"Well, it's just that I really want to be . . ." She waves her hand in the air like a magician. "I want to be au-*then*-tic."

"So? I don't understand how I can help. Wouldn't Michael be better?"

"No. He can't help me. Not like *you* can. Michael has . . . a *family*."

I feel like I've tripped but haven't hit the ground yet.

"Tell me," she says. "What's it like . . . *really* like . . . to be an orphan?"

The ground seems to move.

She leans in. Talking. Talking and talking. Something about me being lucky while I just stand there caught in between wanting to disappear and wanting to help her. I feel around for an answer to her question, but I have none.

I've thought about my mother, of course. I've wondered where she went to and where she's been. But I guess Aimee *is* right; I *was* abandoned . . . and I *am* an orphan. But is it dumb to say that I have never really thought about it like that?

Until now.

Chapter 2

THE BEST ONE YET

"Grammy!" I call, running down our stairs. "Are you almost ready?"

She's in her work uniform, hanging over her jigsaw puzzle. She presses a piece in. "I know you have ants in your pants because Brandy is back at Seaside," she says, standing. "No ants in my pants, though. Another season of cleaning all of those guest cottages." Her hand pats the side of my cheek. "Now, run and get our lunches from the fridge. And don't forget our favorite root beers."

I'm to the kitchen and back in three seconds. "Okay. Let's go!"

We slide into the car. As always, she makes a cross on the dashboard with her finger, looks up through the windshield at the sky, and says a prayer for the car to start. When it does, she pats the dashboard again. "That's a good Darlin'. Starting for your ole Bridget."

She puts it in Drive. "You think it's weird I talk to the car?"

"Only if you think it answers," I say.

She coughs as she laughs. "You hung the moon, you know that?"

That's one of Grammy's best compliments.

At the first stop sign, she looks over at me. "You're like a tick about ready to pop," she says. "Excited to see Brandy, I know."

"I am *so* excited. But a tick ready to pop? Gross . . . No . . . Ew."

"I'll never understand how a girl who loves tornadoes and hurricanes and floods could be scared of a little tick."

"The weather doesn't suck your blood," I say, expecting her to have a comeback, but she just shakes her head.

She flips her turn signal. "So, you talked to Brandy? She and her family staying for the summer as usual?"

"Yeah. She and her mom, anyway."

"Oh my *good*ness, I remember the day you two first met," Grammy says, falling back against the car seat. "Her mom was sweet enough to watch you on a day I had no choice but to bring you along. And you and Brandy, as little as you were, sat side by side in one of those big Adirondack chairs. You've been like peanut butter and jelly ever since."

I laugh. "Grammy. Who wants to be like peanut butter and jelly? That never ends well. For them, anyway."

Grammy shakes her head again as she pulls into a parking spot, and I turn. "Can I go?"

"Yes, but for heaven's sake, look both ways."

As soon as my foot hits the red sidewalk leading into Seaside, I hear Brandy. "Dels!" she calls as she leaps from a picnic table. The place already reeks like sunscreen and burning charcoal, even though it's barely nine o'clock. Summer has officially arrived.

I race across the grass, and we hug and jump around. "Oh my gosh! How are you?" she asks. "I'm soooo happy to see you." Then she steps back. "Wow, Dels. You got tall this year."

"I did?" And then I notice that Brandy looks much older than me, with makeup, a purse, and the kind of clothes you buy in little stores instead of big ones. I feel a little funny about my faded Boston Marathon T-shirt even though it was the greatest tag sale find of the summer last year. But Brandy is smiling, and I am happy to see her.

"I've already pulled out our collecting pails," she says, and that feeling in my stomach melts away. She's the old Brandy.

Since kindergarten, we have collected rocks and shells each summer and glued and painted them to make sculptures.

"But first," I say, pulling at her sleeve, "let's check on the house."

Underneath a huge group of flowering bushes, there is a small stone house that we made the summer before second grade, hoping fairies would move in. That was five summers ago. Now we just check on it first thing.

I drop to my knees and push the branches aside. The house isn't there.

"Where is it?" Brandy asks, crouching next to me.

"I don't know. You think someone took it?"

She laughs. "Well, it wasn't a mobile home, so yeah. Unless the fairies finally showed." She takes a step away.

I crawl through nearby bushes to look for it.

"C'mon," she says. "Let's just head down to the beach."

"Don't you care?" I ask.

"I mean, I wish it were there, Dels, but some little kids probably found it. *So, whatever.*" She tugs at my sleeve. "C'mon. Let's go down to the beach. I have a tan to work on."

A tan? Since when does she care about a tan? I follow, but the little voice that my neighbor Henry always warns me not to ignore—the one people hear in times of danger or when they're about to do something dumb—tells me a cold front is on the horizon. The air is shifting. I'm upset that the house is gone, but I'm mostly worried that Brandy couldn't care less.

We grab the pails, and when she runs, I do, too. The

Fiesters have an old red pail and a blue pail that Mrs. Fiester and her brother used on the Cape a million years ago. They're made of scratched-up metal with rust along the bottom edges. We use one pail for shells and one for rocks so that the shells don't get broken.

"Okay," she says. "Rocks or shells?"

"You choose." I smile, just happy to be back on Seagull Beach with Brandy. I miss her the rest of the year. We chat once in a while, but it isn't the same. We can't wait until her mother and my grammy let us have our own phones. Although I think I am most excited about the app that tracks global lightning strikes.

We spend the morning hanging out on the jetties, collecting things, and having a couple of splash fights with our feet. Finally, we get back to the picnic tables and spread everything out and talk about what sculptures we'll make.

Brandy sorts the rocks by size. "So, don't you think this is babyish to still do?"

"Not if we like it."

"Yeah . . . I guess. And at least no one can see us."

I look up at her. "And if they do, who *cares*?"

"Yeah, I guess you're right," she says.

But I know Brandy. Her mouth may agree, but her brain is thinking something totally different.

Chapter 3

MADRE SEAL

Brandy's mom leans outside and calls to her. "Honey! We have to leave in a few minutes for our appointments."

Brandy yells okay, and I feel sorry for her. "Bummer," I say. "You going to the dentist or something?"

She smiles. "No, my mom and I are getting mani-pedis."

My next-door neighbor Esme gets those, so I know what they are, but I've never had one. It's more likely that Grammy would take me out on a raft in the middle of a nor'easter.

Brandy waves as they go, and I have to swallow an empty feeling I haven't known before as they disappear around the corner.

I'm an orphan. Like Aimee says. No mother. No father.

I never used to think about this. And I never used to worry, either. But now that I've started to, I wonder what

People won't move fast enough for the officer. Leaning forward. Taking pictures. "Honey," a mom says to her daughter in a loud whisper. "Just take a few steps closer to the seal and smile."

The officer becomes a wall, stepping into the line of people with her arms out like she can fly. "No, ma'am. Move back now." I admire how she sounds nice but says *don't mess with me* at the same time.

The line moves, but my feet step forward without my say-so. The seal is small. Is it sick? Is it going to die? The officer eyes me, and I step back with the others.

A boy nearby speaks Spanish. I don't remember much Spanish from school, but he uses the word *madre. That*, I remember, is "mother."

The officer sticks wooden stakes into the sand and ties neon tape around each to create a giant square of bright tape around the seal. "This is very common," she says. "A mother will sometimes leave her pup on the beach while she hunts. The baby is left here on the sand. Safe. Away from the great whites who hunt *them* each summer."

Relief washes over me. The seal pup is okay.

I look toward the rolling waves and wonder where Madre Seal is. How does she remember where she's left her baby on this beach that stretches all along the southern coast of Cape Cod?

"Please do not cross the tape," the officer calls to the crowd. "If Mom sees people too close to her baby, she may leave her behind."

My mind gets stuck on the two words *her baby*. Not *the* baby or *a* baby but *her* baby.

The officer turns and seems to speak only to me. "But don't worry. The mom always comes back."

I look toward the ocean. If only that were true.

• • •

I walk down the beach away from all the people because they make me feel squirrely. And all the way down Seagull Beach, I drag those thoughts of the abandoned pup.

And I wonder if it wonders.

The wet sand squishes up between my toes as I walk. But soon the quietness is interrupted by excited voices carried on the wind. I turn to see that the officer has moved everyone much farther away from the neon tape. All of the noise and pointing toward the ocean tells me there is something to see, so I sprint back, running where the water meets the sand. When I get close enough, I see what looks like a black ball floating in the water. The head of Madre Seal.

The baby seal scurries toward the sea like a fat black inchworm. Under the neon tape. Toward the waves. In the water, Madre Seal swims back and forth, back and forth, and I can feel her worry about all of these people near her baby. But still . . . she is there.

There.

I am surprised at how relieved I am to see her. As the baby hits the water, Madre Seal leaps and dives. Leaps and dives.

And then the most surprising thing happens. I start to cry. Not the kind of cry that you can squelch and swallow but the kind where your whole body knows how you feel. And it's right then that I realize that when people say you can't miss something you've never known . . . Well, that simply isn't true.

Chapter 4

BROKEN

I run barefoot from the sandy beach, in and out of the small neighborhoods, all the way to our house. I push open the front door and stumble in.

Grammy's watching *The Price Is Right* and leans to the side to look around me when I plant myself in front of the TV.

"Grammy. I have to ask you something."

"Oh my goodness, honey bunch. Are you *ever* going to wear shoes?" she asks, shaking her head. "Go get the cream and bandages and let me fix that for you."

I look down and see my foot is bleeding. I hadn't even noticed I'd cut it.

"*Grammy,*" I say, the shrillness of my voice startling me. "Please. *Please* tell me about my mom. I know you don't like to talk about her. But I need to know what she was like.

Did she sound like *me*? Was she a runner? Did she love root beer?"

Grammy looks like the time she got a shock from plugging in the toaster.

"And who is my dad? What's his name?"

"Oh, I'm sorry, baby. I would tell you if I knew, but Mellie never told me."

That hurts.

"Well, then," I ask, stepping forward, "why did she go? Tell me the *truth* about my mom."

"Oh, Delsie. Why do you want to talk about all that? There's no reason to stir up sad things."

"I know you don't like to talk about her, but I just don't understand why."

"The same reason I don't drink coffee," Grammy says. "Because it hurts my stomach and it makes me feel all terrible inside, and *why* would I do anything that makes me feel like *that*?"

"I know it makes you sad to talk about her. I know. But I think if I just *knew* stuff, it would be better. *Not* knowing is the worst feeling in the world. Not knowing your mom is like not knowing your birthday. Everyone should know that."

Sadness flashes across her face and then she pats the couch next to her. "Come sit with your ole grammy. Let's find out who'll win the Showcase Showdown. A lady bid on two cars. *Two!*" She holds up two fingers. She's wide-eyed and smiling, and I know I won't learn anything about my mother.

"Later," I say, walking past her.

I have no intention of going back, and I know she won't come looking during a Showcase Showdown unless the house is on fire. And even that's questionable.

My bedroom door squeaks as it closes. I sit on my bed and reach for the picture of my mother in a frame covered in sweet candy pieces and glitter. A picture I have said good night to since Papa Joseph taught me to pray.

My mind whirls like a storm system. Questions break and bruise. Smash and spin.

And I can't shake seeing the seal and wondering how it can be so much luckier than me. My fingertips turn white from squeezing the frame too hard. The words "it's not *fair*" rise up and out of me, and glass bounces on the floor when I throw the picture. And looking at the pieces, I am shattered, too.

The broken pieces remind me of Grammy's puzzles. Although I've never understood the point of puzzles—and why you'd sit for hours trying to put a picture that's been broken into hundreds of pieces back together. Plus, when you have the cover, you know exactly what you'll get in the end.

I guess I am sort of like a pile of puzzle pieces that have been dumped on the floor. But I can't put the pieces together because I don't know what the picture on the box is. I don't know who I am—or how many pieces I might be missing. And since Aimee shone a light on something that was in front of me all this time, it makes me wonder what else I'm not seeing.

Looking at the broken pieces, I feel broken, too.

OLIVE OIL

Our neighborhood is at the end of a dirt road that most people think is a driveway. It's lollipop shaped, with the road being the stick that leads to a circle of four houses—three that are lived in and one that's been empty for years.

We have shade all year from scrub pines that look like the crooked trees in a Dr. Seuss book. But in the middle of the circle is a regular pine tree that towers over everything else. It's called Olive's Tree after one of our neighbors, though I don't know why, other than that she loves it and has been here longer than any of us.

Finally, there is a sign as you enter our little neighborhood that says NO DUMPING, and as you leave, a faded, moldy sign reads THANK YOU.

Grammy says it means "thank you for having visited."

Olive says it means "thank you for leaving."

Now Olive is standing at our door.

Olive Tinselly reminds me of a hurricane. Spinning and stormy and gaining strength as she barrels forth. But like the eye of the storm, she has times when she is calm. Even sunny. On Olive's stormy days, Grammy says we need to be extra good to her. That she's had a lot of loss and sadness. But Olive doesn't seem sad to me. She just seems angry.

When I open the door, I can tell by the shape of her mouth that it's a stormy day. "Is your grammy at home?"

Grammy gets up from her puzzle and steps next to me. "Hello there, Olive. Beautiful evening," she says like she's letting Olive know.

"We *have* to do something about Henry," she spits. "This time he's gone too far."

What? I wonder. *Gone too far? Henry?*

"Did you see what he's done?"

"Well, jeepers crow, Olive," Grammy says. "With Esme off caring for her father and him working full-time and taking care of Ruby by himself, I can't imagine he's had *time* to do anything that would cause any harm."

"Come see with your own eyes, then!"

I hear lovely clinking sounds as we step outside. Mrs. Tinselly points up into a tree in Henry's yard and snaps, "*Look* at that! I think he's lost his mind for real this time. Why would anyone do such a crazy thing?"

Esmarelda "Esme" Lasko's silver spoons are hanging in

the tree, tied there with white string. The tinkling sounds are the spoons hitting each other in the breeze.

"I think it's beautiful," I say.

Olive holds up her finger and opens her mouth to talk.

Grammy steps forward. "Now, Olive. Quit sputtering. Every pancake has two sides. There's probably a darn good reason for this."

First," Olive begins, "Esme paints the house bright red. For goodness' sake, it looks like a fire truck. Not to mention her covering the front of their house with all of those ridiculous metal lizards. I know they remind her of home, but here on the Cape it's silly . . ."

Just then, the screen door swings open and Henry steps onto his porch. "To what do I owe the pleasure of such sweet company?" He winks at me.

"Henry Lasko! What have you *done*?" Olive demands.

"Mighty nice to see you, too, Olive. Lovely day." He pretends to lift a hat to greet her.

Ruby comes through the front door and wraps both of her arms around her daddy's legs and stands on his feet. But it's the way she looks up at him. I've seen this a million times, but this is the first time it's hit me in the stomach. It would be nice to have a dad like Henry.

He puts his hand on top of Ruby's head and glances at the spoons. "This was Ruby's idea, actually. She misses her mom and says the spoons sound like her mom's laughter."

I realize that's true.

"It's been hard." He motions toward his daughter with his head. "Esme's dad is pretty sick, so she won't be back for a while."

I think of Esme's collection of spoons and her wall of teacups and how she lets me choose whatever cup I want when she has me over for tea. In the summer the tea is iced and served in vintage Strong Shoulder mason jars.

Esme always gives me one of those spoons hanging in the tree to stir it, and we drink with our pinkies in the air and laugh. Pretending to be fancier people than we are. My stomach aches thinking about her. And I realize how much I have missed Esme, too.

After staring at Olive for a few moments, Henry looks at me and says, "And speaking of big fish—Delsie! You should have seen the whopper we pulled in today!"

"Henry Lasko!" Olive complains. "Don't you pull that on me."

When Henry doesn't like what Olive is saying, he'll say "speaking of . . ." and then change the subject completely. Olive hates that. She'd rather fight, I think.

"It was a striper," Henry continues, "but I'd never seen one like it. It was worth a chunk of change, but to be honest, it'd have broken my heart to keep it. So I let him go."

"Henry! You *did*n't!" Grammy says.

"I know. Don't tell Esme. But he'd lived such a long

time, I didn't feel like I had the right to put him on someone's plate." He rolls back on his heels a bit. "Actually, he would have filled a *lot* of plates."

"That's a bunch of hooey!" Olive snaps. "What kind of fisherman are you? Poor Joseph McHill is probably shaking his head up there in heaven, having left you his boat when God took him."

Henry and I lock eyes, and he winks at me again. "Papa Joseph would have found a way to save that beautiful fish *and* make money." He looks up and takes a breath. "You know, every day as I head out of Chatham Harbor, I look to the sky and thank Joseph for leaving me the *Reel of Fortune*. It's the best boat on the Cape." Henry steps toward me and messes my hair a bit. "Aw, he was a good man and a good friend, your papa was. I miss him, too."

Olive starts talking about the spoons, but Henry interrupts her. "Speaking of Ruby, we better get back inside." He leaves, chuckling to himself.

When Henry's door closes, Grammy takes a deep breath, staring at his house. "You're absolutely right, Olive," Grammy says. "Something *must* be done."

Olive gives Grammy one big, satisfied nod. "*Finally*. Some *sense*."

"I know just the thing. Henry needs a bit of baked goods," Grammy says with a grin. "Maybe some brownies. Or some of that blueberry pie he likes." She turns to me. "What do you think, Delsie?"

"Wh-wh-what?" Olive stammers. "That won't solve a *thing*. What *about* . . . the *spoons*?"

"No spoon on earth has ever felt lonely or forgotten, Olive. But Henry? We must remind him and Ruby that we are their neighbors and friends." She leans forward and looks her in the eye. "And, Olive, aren't you just the sweetest thing to bring this to our attention?"

"Well, that's not exactly—"

Grammy interrupts, "You know, you *could* help us bake, Olive."

"Well, I . . . I mean, I don't know . . . I have a lot of things to do."

"Well, if you change your mind, don't you hesitate to give us a yell, now."

Olive has that look about her. Like she wants to come but won't let herself. I also know that while we're baking, Grammy will send me over to borrow something we don't even need. To give Olive another chance to come.

I smile to myself. Grammy's always saying that when people throw rocks, you can either build walls or bridges. Grammy has always been a bridge builder.

Chapter 6

LIGHTNING BOY

When I show up at Seaside the next day, Brandy is sitting on the kitchen counter, talking to her mom.

"Hey, Dels," she greets me, wiping her chin as strawberry juice runs down it. I notice her fingernails. Bright blue. Her toenails are red. I glance at her mom. Same colors.

"Looks like the mani-pedi went well," I say. My smile makes me feel like my face will crack. And I feel guilty. You're not supposed to feel jealous of a friend, are you?

Brandy turns back toward the counter so I can't see what she is doing. Then she spins around wearing new sunglasses. Aviators, I think.

"You like?" she asks. "We got them yesterday."

"Yeah, they're cool," I say.

"Surprise!" she yells, pulling out a second pair. "We got some for you, too!"

Then all of a sudden, I'm happy. Happy that they thought of me when they were out. "Thanks." I smile and slip them on my face, and I like the way they look in the reflection of her glasses. I like the way they make me feel, too. We high-five.

I turn. "Thank you, Mrs. Fiester," I say. "They are really cool."

"You're very welcome, Delsie. Brandy seemed to think you two had to have matching ones." She turns back to the counter, laughing.

Brandy and I head outside wearing our sunglasses and sit at one of the picnic tables. The new guy in charge of taking care of the place is fixing the lid on one of the grills. He nods at us. Grammy told me about him. She said that he seems to be able to fix anything that either God or man has made, but he isn't one for conversation.

I turn to Brandy, pushing my glasses up my nose. "So what should we do? You want to build a sandcastle with a moat? See how long the castle can last? Deepest moat in Cape history."

She looks at her nails. "I can't dig in the sand with a new manicure," she tells me.

"We could go clamming?"

She shakes her head. "Too messy."

Too *messy*? That's something I've never heard from her before.

"Wait! I know. Let's make a new fairy house."

"Are you *kidding*?"

"*What?* It would be fun," I say.

"Right after finger painting and Play-Doh?"

When I look down, my sunglasses fall off. As I bend over to pick them up, I hear her sigh.

"Is Aimee around?" she asks.

"No, we're not going to see her much this summer," I say. "She got the lead in the Cape Playhouse musical."

She turns her head quick. "The *play*house? *Seriously?*"

I laugh a bit. "Yeah, I know. Rehearsals start this week. It's a big deal for her—she's playing Annie."

"That's cool," Brandy says, but she looks bored as she flops down on the grass and picks out clovers. "So is your oldest living bird still alive?"

I laugh. "Yeah."

"*Please* tell me your bird's name is still Birdie."

I laugh again. "Yep. You know I was in diapers when I named the thing."

"Last year, then?"

I give her a little shove. "You're hilarious. Well . . . you want to go for a run?" I ask.

"Me? No way. Plus it's too hot." She looks up at me. "So did you ever join track?"

"No. But I've been training for a 5K in Yarmouth this September. It will raise money for heart disease."

"Aw, is that for your papa?"

26

I nod, thinking about the day Grammy told me he'd had a heart attack. About how Brandy stood next to me then, and put her arm around my shoulders at his funeral. About how the world has felt like a different place ever since. I look out at the clouds forming over the ocean. I can tell that rain is coming.

Brandy tickles my feet. "Are you wearing shoes now that you run more?"

"Nope. I do everything possible to avoid shoes."

She looks at my feet more closely. "Eww. Your feet look like they were in a knife fight. You walk over glass, or what?"

"Probably," I tell her. "But I don't remember feeling anything."

"Well, you're braver than me. I love my sneakers."

"Do you still sleep with them on?"

She gives *me* a little shove. "That was forever ago."

"Fourth grade wasn't *that* long ago. Now, *that's* weird. Admit it."

"No way. Never." Then she looks at me over her sunglasses. "So what's the plan? Should we go for a swim? We have new boogie boards."

I look back over the ocean. "We can't go swimming," I say. "A storm is coming in."

"The weather says cloudy but no rain."

I realize that I forgot to check our weather station at home today. But I'm pretty sure I'm still right. "No. Rain is coming. Those are cumulonimbus clouds. Besides . . . can't you smell it?"

"*Smell* it?"

"Yeah, smell it. Seriously? You don't smell the rain? It's beautiful."

"I think you've baked your brain in the sun, that's what I think."

Soon a light rain begins to fall, and Mrs. Fiester yells, "Oh no! Girls! Please run down to the beach and collect my towels."

Brandy looks at me like I have special powers, and we leap up. By the time we've taken just three steps, the rain has started to come down like God pulled the plug on his bathtub. "You were so right!" Brandy yells as she runs. We laugh, running across the grass as tiny water bombs drop from the sky. The rain doesn't just fall. It's driven, carried by the winds. Out over the sea, the dark clouds flicker like heaven is about to lose power.

At the top of the stairs, I spot some sheet lightning in the distance, which is one of my favorite kinds. I stop to count so I'll know how far away the storm is. Five seconds in between seeing the lightning and hearing the thunder means it's one mile away. As my counting reaches five, the thunder cracks and rumbles above, shooting vibrations through the wooden steps. The storm is a mile away.

Brandy squeals, running down the steps, and I follow.

She scurries around gathering towels and flinging them over her shoulder.

But I am stuck in place. Staring at a boy wearing black jeans and a long-sleeved black T-shirt even though it's summer. He stands at the water's edge, looking out over the ocean.

"Hey!" I yell. "It's dangerous to have your feet in the water during a lightning storm!"

"Dels! C'mon!" Brandy yells, bolting up the stairs in a frenzy.

There's a flash. Then I count. After four seconds, the crack of thunder sounds like a giant breaking the sky in two. The storm is closer.

"Hey!" I yell to the boy. "Did you hear me? Get out of the water!"

The boy lifts one foot and steps back.

He never turns around to look at me, and I am tempted to go over to see his face.

Brandy yells again. "Delsie! What are you doing? *C'mon!*"

I spin on one foot and run with her, but with every step, my brain asks another question about the boy dressed completely in black who stands at the water's edge in the middle of a lightning storm.

Chapter 7

PLAYING GAMES

"Jeepers crow!" Grammy says, coming up behind me at Seaside Heaven. "I need your help with one of the rooms. The people turned the furniture upside down and asked to have the undersides of things cleaned. I don't think it's a joke because they left a hefty tip . . ."

I help Grammy with the cleaning, but turning the furniture back over is hard. So she calls the office and asks for help.

Soon the new guy who helps take care of the place shows up. Behind him is the boy in black.

Grammy extends her hand. "Bridget McHill. Thanks so much for coming over. I don't know what these people were thinking . . ."

The guy reaches out and shakes Grammy's hand. "Yeah,

you never know," he says. He turns to me. "I'm Gusty Gale. This is my son, Ronan."

"Gusty Gale?" I blurt out. "That's the best name ever. I mean *ever* in the history of the universe and the world. I totally love it."

Father's and son's eyebrows pop up at the same time. Like they practiced it.

"It's way better than plain old Delsie McHill," I explain.

Grammy scoffs. "Delsie McHill, why, your name is like a song, honey bunch. Gusty Gale . . . is . . ." She glances his way. "Well, very nice, too." Grammy turns a bit red.

"Well, thank you both," he says, chuckling. "My legal name is Sherman, but I go by Gusty."

"Oh, I don't blame you," I say. "Sherman is an old guy's name. But Gusty's a guy who treats everyone to fish and chips on Friday night. It's much better!"

Grammy bursts out laughing. "You can see that we always know what Delsie is thinking."

"No worries," Gusty says. "I prefer people who say what's on their mind."

"Well, no worries there," Grammy says.

The boy finally speaks. "You do know what a gale is, right? And what Gusty Gale would mean?"

"Oh yeah! A stormy storm. He's two words that kind of mean the same thing. Like soaking wet."

"Yeah, well . . . some say I *am* pretty stormy," Gusty says.

I turn to Grammy. "Maybe I need a weather nickname, too. How about Muggy McHill? Or Monsoon McHill?"

The first few notes of a song begin on Grammy's radio. I recognize it right away.

"'The Wreck of the *Edmund Fitzgerald*.' My papa Joseph loved that song," I blurt out. "I bet the captain in this song was named Gusty Gale."

"Well," Gusty begins, "considering that's a song about a ship and crew that met their end, I hope not."

The boy, Ronan, eyes me the way you would an alien stepping out of its spaceship and asking for pie.

Gusty stuffs his hands in his pockets. "I've never lost a crew member, thank God, but I have lost a fishing boat to a storm. The *Inafundável*. Was a shame, it was. Haven't forgiven myself. Never will, I imagine."

His son gives him a puzzled look. I guess he didn't know that.

"Well, I'm glad you're okay. My papa used to say that anything made by man can be replaced, but not so much with things made by God."

He nods slowly. "Yup. That's true for sure."

Then he takes a deep breath, lifts his head, and taps the side of his son's arm. He points with his chin toward the room, and Gusty and Ronan begin to flip the furniture back over for us. Grammy reaches for the tip the customers left and holds out a five-dollar bill to them.

Ronan reaches out, but Gusty steps forward. "Naw. That's okay. You keep that." He nods once at his son, and they both give a wave and turn to go. Ronan glances back quick. Not at me but at Grammy.

• • •

I find Brandy before reaching the beach. She is sitting at a picnic table, playing cards with a girl I don't know.

"Hey," I say. "Sorry I'm late. I was helping Grammy clean." I look at the girl and hope she isn't staying in that room.

The girl only looks at me for a second.

"Hey, Dels. This is Tressa. Her mom works with my mom. They are renting a house a few blocks from here for the summer."

"That's cool," I say.

"It's your turn." The girl stares at Brandy.

"What are you playing?" I ask.

"Gin rummy." Brandy picks up a fan of cards and glances at me. I know that look. She's got lots of points.

"Can I play?" I ask.

"Sure," Brandy says.

"Wait," Tressa says. "We're playing to five hundred. How can she jump in in the middle?"

"It'll be okay," Brandy says. "I'll give her half my points."

"Thanks," I say, falling onto the bench next to Brandy.

Tressa tosses her cards down. "Never mind. I was getting tired of this game anyway." She swings her legs around and stands. "So this is the famous Cape Cod, right? What do you all do around here, anyway?"

"Well, we *whale* watch for one thing," Brandy says, bumping my shoulder with hers. "Delsie! My mom is taking us on a whale watch for my birthday on Friday. You can come, right?"

"Are you kidding? Yes! Aaaand . . . I've already got your present—something no one else will get you, for sure."

"Should I worry?" she asks, smiling.

"Maybe a little," I say, locking eyes with her. Although I know she'll be happy with her gift, I'm the one who thinks it's kind of creepy.

Tressa rolls her eyes. "Well, that's real exciting. And what *else* do you do here?"

I open my mouth to say something to Brandy, but she jumps up before I can get it out and follows Tressa down to the beach.

The little voice warns me.

Chapter 8

A LIAR AND A THIEF

The next day, when I arrive at Seaside, Brandy and Tressa are heading to Sundae School, a fancy ice cream place. They ask me to go, so I find Grammy and ask if I can have some money.

"That place is too rich for my blood," she says, never taking her eyes off the sink she is scrubbing. "You can get some out of our freezer for a fraction of the cost."

"*Please?*"

She sighs. "There's a five-dollar bill in my wallet. Although you know it won't get you much there."

"Thanks, Grammy," I say, taking the money and running to find Brandy and Tressa. Hoping they haven't left already.

Tressa stares at my feet. "*Shoes?*" she asks.

"I'm good without."

Brandy laughs. "Delsie doesn't believe in shoes."

"Great. Like Tarzan. Good for you," Tressa mumbles. "My cousin doesn't wear shoes, either. She's a year old."

Brandy seems to be thinking about Tressa's comment. So I give her a gentle shove. "Remember how I got you to give up shoes last summer? You bounced around the hot pavement like a ball in a pinball machine."

"Yeah, because I'm *normal*," Brandy says.

"Why would anyone wear shoes on the Cape? It's like wearing a wet suit in the bathtub."

"Yeah, Delsie." Tressa laughs. "It's just like that."

I sigh.

When we finally get there, I swing open the door. I love the ice cream here, but my favorite part of the place is the player piano. For a quarter it will play all by itself.

"Excuse me, miss." The shop's manager has spotted me. "You'll have to wait outside for your friends."

I was hoping to get away with it, as the manager is usually busy. Today is unlucky.

"Oh," I mumble.

Tressa is already in line, and Brandy rushes over. "What are you doing? C'mon," she says, darting her eyes between me and Tressa.

"I can't come in because I don't have shoes. So . . . so, I guess I'll wait outside." I hand her the five-dollar bill. "Get me a small sweet cream with a boatload of jimmies. Chocolate."

She half smiles. "*Yeah,* I *know.*"

I head back outside and watch them through the window, and I see exactly what I'm afraid to see. Brandy. Laughing like she's with the best, most interesting friend in the world. She used to look at me that way.

I stare at my dirty feet. Then back up at my reflection. I don't like what I see and wish I could go to a hairdresser instead of having Grammy cut my hair over the kitchen sink.

Then in the reflection I see something I don't expect—Ronan, the boy from the beach. He is still wearing black jeans and a black long-sleeved shirt, although the sleeves are pushed up past his elbows. He is drinking a milkshake and doesn't seem to bother breathing as he does.

I turn around. "Hey."

I hear the noise of a straw sucking more air than milkshake. He turns, lifts the cup into the air, and lobs it into the garbage can. Finally he turns to me. "What do you *want?*"

"Nothing. Just talking."

"Well, you don't need to talk to me," he tells me. "Why does everyone on Cape Cod talk to strangers?"

Locals call it "the Cape." *Cape Cod* is only for the tourists' T-shirts. "You're not from around here, are you?"

"No, Detective. I'm not." He looks up at me. "Has anyone ever told you and your friends that you remind them of great hammerhead sharks?"

This is obviously not a compliment.

"They only swim in shallow waters." He laughs as he leaves.

A familiar voice calls my name. I turn, and Aimee and Michael are coming across the parking lot.

Aimee gives me a quick hug. "You here alone?"

"No, I'm with Brandy and another girl."

"Brandy? Cool. Does another girl have an actual name or is she supremely unlucky?"

"Her name is Tressa. But it's me who's supremely unlucky." I motion toward the door. "They're inside."

"Ha!" Michael says. "They wouldn't let you in because of the feet, right?"

"Still haven't joined civilization, huh?" Aimee smiles.

"Civilization is overrated, I think."

"Yeah," Michael agrees. "Why should you have to wear shoes? People's hands are probably worse. Not like everyone has to wear gloves."

I shrug and hope we still aren't discussing my dirty bare feet when Tressa comes back out.

"So how come you're not rehearsing?" I ask.

"Well, we have time off *once* in a while. We looked for you at Seaside. Your grammy told us you were here."

"Hey, guys," Brandy says, rushing over when she sees them. "I hear you're big stars this summer."

Brandy gives them both a hug. Tressa stands behind her, looking Michael and Aimee over.

"Well, I don't know about stardom," Aimee says.

"Not *yet*," I say, and she smiles.

Brandy hands me my ice cream.

"Oh!" Aimee says. "Can I *please*?"

I nod, and she scoops some with her finger. Tressa looks like she's been stuck with a pin.

Someone yells, and I turn to see the manager arguing with Ronan. He's standing on the running board of the shop's antique ice cream truck with the giant sign that says DO NOT TOUCH.

"I've told you before to stay off of that truck," the man shouts. "I won't tell you again."

"Well, *that's* good news."

The man's eyebrows knit together as he steps toward the boy.

"Yeah, yeah," Ronan says. He gets down and backs away. "I'm *going*."

Tressa scoffs. "What's his problem, anyway?"

"I don't know," Brandy says. "He lives at Seaside Heaven with his father, the new fix-it guy. He doesn't talk much."

I'm just about to tell them he spoke to me when I remember what he said. I look over at Tressa, thinking of hammerhead sharks.

"Well." Tressa sits up straighter. "*I* think someone ought to tell him it's summer and that maybe he should change his clothes."

"Yeah," Michael says. "Because we can tell *every*thing about him from his *clothes*."

Tressa shoots him a look. He obviously doesn't care, and I envy him.

"I feel sorry for him," Brandy says.

"Why?" Tressa darts back. "He is *not* a nice person."

"How do *you* know?" Aimee asks.

Tressa looks at her like she's a fool.

I have to admit I'm not sure that he's all that nice, but the little voice tells me to keep quiet about him.

"Hel*lo*?" Tressa begins. "Did you just see him? I heard he's always in trouble and he stole stuff from a room when his father went in to fix something. And he's a liar, too, because he said he didn't do it."

I want to ask how she's so sure, but I have a feeling that telling Tressa she may be wrong about something is like poking a bear with a fork.

So, as she reports on all of the things she's "heard," I stare at him. Ronan is now leaning against a fence in the parking lot with his fists tucked underneath his armpits. I notice the way he pushes his chin forward like he's ready for a fight . . . while his face is so sad.

Tressa continues. "I don't know. You should complain,

Brandy. You have to live with him at Seaside. Who knows what he'll do?"

Brandy doesn't say much. In fact, she doesn't say anything at all, which isn't like the Brandy I've always known.

Michael turns to Aimee. "We should get going."

She nods, I hug them both, and they head across the parking lot.

"Let's go back to the beach," Brandy says, and I nod.

As we leave, I keep my eyes on the boy in black, who is possibly both a liar and a thief.

Chapter 9

MORE THAN A FLUKE

I was more excited about the whale watch before I found out Tressa was coming.

I think about the gift I got for Brandy and how much she's going to like it as we board the boat with Mrs. Fiester.

I run up the stairs to the top decks. Tressa and Brandy follow. The boat is filled with blue benches. There are safety ring buoys hanging on the walls. Having been trained by Papa and Henry, I look for the lifeboats, too, and see they are stacked on top of the cabin.

When the boat takes off, I can feel the motor rumbling through the deck. Brandy's looking at Tressa's phone, and the two of them are laughing at some video. I want to join in but know Tressa won't like that. And I'd rather look at the ocean anyway.

Huge waves rise and fall, rise and fall, like a slow-motion

watery seesaw. The boat bobs up and down with each wave. It makes me feel tiny. I call to Brandy to come look.

Brandy and Tressa arrive to see the enormous fluke of a whale as it dives. The scientist on board tells us that the fluke, or tail, of a whale is like a person's fingerprint. Each one is different. I turn to Brandy and say, "That's so cool!" but she is gone. Those two are already sitting on the bench, watching more videos.

But now we are surrounded by whales. Like most people on the boat, I run from port to starboard and back again to see the ones that breach the surface and wave their flippers. I'm pointing with the tourists and as excited as a six-year-old.

When I glance back at Brandy and Tressa, they are laughing again. And I realize they are taking a video of me.

• • •

I am relieved when we finally get back to Seaside. The day hasn't been what I hoped, although the whales were great. I just wish I had seen them with the old Brandy.

But I am excited to give her her present. My wrapping job is not super neat, but I think it looks cool. Grammy saves up comics from the *Boston Globe* to use as wrapping paper. She says even if you bought the *Globe* just for that reason, you'd save a fortune on wrapping. I've always thought it was pretty clever.

Brandy's gift was hard to wrap because of its

shape—underneath is a clown. I think that clowns are freaky, but Brandy loves them and always tells me about her collection back home. When I found an old ceramic one at a tag sale, I knew it was the perfect present. And I've named her Edwina after a clown we saw at the carnival last summer, who juggled and told dumb jokes. Back when we could laugh at dumb stuff.

I hand Brandy the package.

"Pfft," Tressa says. "Nice wrapping paper."

Clearly she's being sarcastic, but I try to focus on Brandy and watching her open the present. As I'd hoped, her face lights up.

"Do you like it?" I ask.

"I do, Dels! She's great. *Thank* you!"

"You're welcome. I was so excited when I found it at a tag sale. Doesn't she remind you of the clown we saw last summer?"

"*Wait*," Tressa interrupts. "You bought her a used birthday present?"

"It's new to her," I say.

"Look," she says, leaning toward me, "it's either used or it isn't. They don't sell new stuff at tag sales."

Brandy turns red.

I try to brighten. "Her name is Edwina. Like that clown we met in Hyannis."

"Of course it is," Tressa sighs. Then she pushes a box toward Brandy. "Here. Open *my* present. My *new* present."

Brandy opens it.

A pair of sunglasses that look just like Tressa's. "Oh!" Brandy says. "These are *just* what I needed!"

Chapter 10

IT'S A HARD-KNOCK LIFE

I spend the morning lying on the beach with Tressa and Brandy, and I try to pretend that I like it. We set up towels and just lie there like bacon. I hate it. If I'm at the beach, I'd rather collect stuff or run or be in the water. Lying in one place for this long is for bedtime or getting over the flu. So I guess that's why I doze off. And when I wake up, it's because someone is kicking my leg. Not hard but still kicking it.

"Brandy, cut it out," I say. Opening my eyes and looking back over my shoulder, I see Ronan standing over me. "What do you *want*?"

"I'm guessing you don't want the word *boring* written across your back in white letters."

"What are you talking about?" I jump to my feet and hear Tressa laughing. Brandy punches her the way a friend does, kidding around. The way she used to punch me.

I'm still confused. Write on my back in white letters? This kid is bonkers. "Listen," I say. "I don't know what you—"

"They wrote on your back with sunscreen," he interrupts. "They wrote *boring* in giant letters. I don't know how long you've been lying there, but if you burned . . . or tanned . . . or whatever . . ." He takes a step back and turns to leave. "Anyway, I did you a favor by waking you up."

Tressa laughs, but it sounds fake. Like someone in a play who isn't very good at acting. Brandy and I lock eyes for a second, but she looks away quick. So she was in on it. I feel like I've been punched.

The boy is a ways down the beach now. Throwing rocks.

I reach for my back and feel gobs of sunscreen. I scoop my T-shirt off the sand, shake it hard, and put it on. "Thanks a lot," I say as I trudge away.

I look at my watch. It's been a long time. I worry I'll have that BORING sign on my back. A sign I can't wash off. This is just *great*.

Walking across the lawn, I think to look for Grammy, but she'll know something is wrong by looking at me. I'm way too humiliated to explain.

Loneliness rises all around me like fog in the early morning. And I realize how much I miss the friends who don't make my stomach hurt.

I know Aimee and Michael are practicing today, and so I decide to go to the playhouse.

It'll be a good reminder that I still have decent friends in the world.

And I guess I'd like to see what a play about an orphan looks like.

• • •

The Cape Playhouse looks like a barn filled with rows of benches. It's dark and smells like a hot attic. I count seven ceiling fans spinning above.

The rehearsal is what I expect—a bunch of kids singing, "It's a hard-knock life."

A hard-knock life, huh? All these actors with their mothers waiting for them outside in their cars. After practice, they'll all go to the beach or out to lunch at one of those fancy places where you can't go barefoot like you can at my favorite place, Saucepan Lynn's.

The worst thing, unfortunately, is Aimee. She can sing, that's for sure. But she's loud and chirpy as she sings about not mattering to anyone. The kinds of feelings *I* think you'd squeeze and squash, not be singing about with outstretched arms and showing every tooth you have.

All of this weighs on my heart until I am jolted by a yell.

A tall, rectangular woman steps into the spotlight. "I have *told* you before," she says to an actor about my age. "You will refer to me as Madam. You will refer to me as Madam Schofield. If I'm in an exceptionally patient mood, you may call me Madam Katrinka. But you will *never* refer to me as a pronoun. I am not a *she* or a *her* like any other *she* or *her*. Do we understand each other?"

He answers, "Yes, Madam Schofield." He sounds tired of saying it.

She would be a perfect villain in a Disney movie. I laugh.

She whips around, squinting as she peers into the audience. Then she bellows, "Bring up the house lights!" And as if God flipped a switch, I am standing under what feels like a hot sun.

"Something humorous?" she asks, trudging down the steps.

"Hey, I just—"

"Did you not *hear* me?" she says as if I am half a mile away. "That's *Madam*. I am not a *hey*."

I see surprise on the faces of Michael and Aimee. Perhaps a little fear as well.

"Why did you laugh?" she demands.

"Oh . . . *Madam* . . . I had just remembered a joke and—"

She interrupts. "Please share it with us, then."

Oh no. My mind scrambles for a joke, but I can only think of a riddle. "Well, what would you do if you had to escape from a room with no doors or windows and only had a plastic knife and a peanut butter and jelly sandwich—"

She pushes her palm in my direction like she's closing an invisible door. "Never mind," she bellows. She darts back up the steps, waving her arm, and all the kids onstage scurry into a line. Must be nice to have that kind of power.

I take a seat on a bench in the back, careful to be quiet.

There are a lot of things in the play I remember from the movie.

I am surprised to learn that Rooster, Miss Hannigan's mean brother, is played by Michael.

He does okay when he sings "Easy Street," but I can hardly hear him.

Madam Schofield steps onto center stage. "MISTER Poole," she bellows. "Yours is a shallow performance. I simply . . . don't believe you."

"Believe me?" he asks.

"No, I mean I don't believe your *character*. I don't believe that you are him—and *that* is your *job* as an actor. To make us *believe*."

"Well, it's not easy playing this Rooster guy. I'm nothing like him."

"Rubbish!" she snaps.

"What?" Michael is wide-eyed. "He's such a jerk. I would never do the things he does."

She points. "We are all jerks inside. And kind. And smart. We are all thoughtful *and* inconsiderate. We are all polite *and* rude. We are all everything. And I need to see the jerk in you to believe you are Rooster."

Michael's whole face seems to glow like a Christmas bulb.

She steps forward. "Do you mean to tell me that you

have never done an unkind thing? Have never thought a bad thing? Have never said something that hurt someone else?"

"No, I have, I guess."

"To act, you must become someone else. Use the tiny parts of yourself that can relate to your character and make him believable. Adopt his personalities. Adopt his thoughts and feelings and opinions, even if they are not your own. If you can't do that, Mr. Poole, well, you should be scooping ice cream this summer instead of acting."

Michael is silent.

She steps forward and bends down to meet his eyes. "Are you angry at me, Mr. Poole? Wouldn't you like to say something unkind?"

He nods.

"Good," she says, spinning away. "Use those feelings."

Chapter 11

SHUDDER AT THE THOUGHT

On Sunday morning I check my sunburnt back. BORING is still there but not as noticeable as it was last night. Still, I can't wear a bathing suit without a shirt for several more days.

I don't tell Grammy because she would go into orbit. She hates it when people are mean to each other.

I call Aimee. "What are the chances that you and Michael would want to go tag-saling with me? I have to find something."

"Sure! Why not. When are you going?"

"As soon as you can get here. Do you think Michael will want to go?"

"Are you kidding? Michael will do anything to get out of the campground he has to live in. His family had to leave their house for the summer again so the landlord can rent it out to tourists for more money. Just like last year. He's pretty miserable."

"Okay. Well, call him and tell him we'll cheer him up, and to get over here as quick as possible."

"Your grammy would be proud of you getting all worked up over tag sales."

•••

I smell Michael before I see him.

"Well, there are worse things than smelling like s'mores," I joke.

"Maybe. At least the smoke from the campfire keeps mosquitoes away, so I stayed in front of it all night. The tent is crowded, too, so outside is the better of the terrible choices."

"I thought boys liked camping."

His face is stone. "I thought girls liked shoes."

I look down at my feet. "Okay. You got me there."

Aimee arrives in time to hear this exchange. "Touché," she says.

"C'mon, you guys," I say, leading the way. "Time to find some treasures."

"What are you looking for, anyway?" Aimee asks.

I hesitate. "A new frame for . . . a picture."

"A picture of what?" Michael asks.

I swallow. "My mother."

"I thought you didn't know your mother," he says.

When I don't reply, Aimee turns and taps him on the arm. "Hey, maybe she doesn't want to talk about it."

"But it's the truth, right? She *doesn't* know her."

"Michael," Aimee says. "It's her business, and maybe something that bothers her, and she doesn't want a group of people standing around discussing it."

"Well, we're not just any group of people," he says, coming over and putting his arm around my shoulder. "We love Delsie. She's our people. We're her supporting actors in *life*."

I bump shoulders with him. "Thanks, Michael. It does make me sad to talk about it, though. Maybe another time . . ."

Part of me would like to talk to them, but I wonder if Grammy is right—maybe talking about things just stirs up sadness.

I'm grateful that Aimee stepped in like that, though. I've been wondering if she's been curious why I went quiet that day she asked for help with her part, but it seems like she understands. I'm lucky. When the waves are rolling in, my friends are the jetties.

• • •

The first two tag sales are filled with a lot of glass and stuff I wouldn't want.

But I get a good feeling after arriving at the third one and spotting a Strong Shoulder mason jar like we drink iced tea from in the neighborhood.

Aimee calls to me, "Delsie! I found a frame!"

I head over. It's a frame that says CAPE COD and has a seal on it. Another weird coincidence. But I don't want that frame as a reminder, so I say, "What self-respecting Caper would have a frame that says Cape Cod?"

An old guy in a chair says, "Exactly why I'm selling it!" and he laughs like he thinks he's the funniest guy east of the Bourne Bridge.

"I think it's perfect for you," Michael says. "I happen to know that you are a wash-ashore."

"I got here at two days old," I say. "Close enough."

"If you didn't take your first breath on this side of the bridge, then you are not a Caper. You are a wash-ashore."

Aimee smacks him on the arm. "What is *with* you? Lighten up."

"Why? I smell like a house fire," he complains. "I'm in a bad mood."

"I get it," Aimee says. "But living at the campground can't be all bad. You must have *some* fun there."

"Yeah, I guess it could be seen as fun. But then again"—he leans forward and gets in her face—"I'm not a raccoon. Another reason I smell so nice is I hate their showers. I mean, some things are meant to be community. Showers are not one of them."

"They have walls, right?" I ask.

"Sort of. But you don't have to look at other people's feet

when you shower, do you? I *really* don't need to do that. I don't mind sharing. Really I don't. I can share my dessert. A bench. Seriously. I'd rather share a head cold than a shower."

"I know what's really bothering you," Aimee says. "You're mad because Madam Schofield gave you a hard time."

"Which *time*?" he asks.

"O-o-okay. So she gave you a hard time forty-seven times. But it's the Cape Playhouse. It's renowned."

"I just want to act," he says. "I don't care if it's *renowned*."

She rolls her eyes and lets it go.

Michael's head flops back, and he groans. "But the worst part of living at the campground is I'm surrounded by people who think everyone is on vacation like they are. I'm not on *va-ca-tion*. I just get kicked out of my house every summer so our landlord can make more money from summer people."

"I'm sorry, Michael. That's a drag," I say, but he doesn't seem satisfied. I figure I'll give him some time alone while I shop around. "Hey, I'll be back in a bit."

I walk over to a table and find a digital camera. I think of all the family pictures on the Laskos' wall and how we have hardly any. Maybe having a camera would be good.

The camera is marked twenty dollars, which doesn't seem like too much for a digital camera that works. But Grammy would make me eat tuna on toast for a week if I didn't bargain, so I go up to the lady.

"Excuse me, ma'am?"

"Look," she says, "I'll give you a dollar discount right off the bat if you don't call me ma'am again."

"Will you take thirteen dollars if I call you Your Highness?"

Her laughter is so loud it makes *me* laugh.

"Well . . ." She moves forward. "This is a nice camera, but my grandson jammed a screwdriver in this port," she says, pointing. "So you can't plug it into a computer anymore. But you can insert the memory stick into the machines at the store and print them that way."

I can't believe how lucky I am, but I'm careful not to react. So I drop my voice to show some disappointment. Big part of negotiating. "Well, will you take thirteen dollars?"

"Doesn't that seem a bit low?"

I hear someone playing a xylophone behind me and know that it must be Aimee. I turn to see I'm right. And Michael is playing an air guitar.

I reach into my pocket and pull out fifteen one-dollar bills wadded up in a ball. "How about fifteen dollars, with that old jar?" I say, pointing at the Strong Shoulder. I decide against the frame because I don't know if I can put my mom's picture in a seal frame. "That's my final offer. Mostly because that's all I have."

She stares at me. Half smiling.

The xylophone is louder, and Michael is now singing.

"And . . . I'll leave quickly and take my two loud friends with me. If that will help."

She laughs. "Boy, you're a pistol, aren't you?" She leans to the side. "He's a pretty good singer, actually."

"Yeah, they both are. They're going to be in *Annie* at the playhouse. That's Annie and Rooster right there."

"*Real*-ly? That's cool! We have tickets." She looks down at the camera in my hand. "I tell you what," she says. "It's a deal!"

I give her the camera and my ball of ones, and she comes back with a little bag holding the jar wrapped in newspaper and the camera. "I may have thrown something extra in there," she says, winking.

Then she picks up a pencil and pad and walks over to Aimee and Michael. "So I hear you two are local stars. I'd love to have your autographs."

Aimee doesn't even try to hide how happy she is. Michael tries to play it cool, whipping off his name fast, but Aimee's tongue curls around the corner of her mouth as she writes. She's done that forever, anytime she concentrates. It takes her so long, you'd swear she was writing a whole paragraph. But as we leave, she is practically flying.

Walking away, I glance in the bag and see the surprise is the seal frame. My stomach rolls. The reminder I didn't want is now mine.

But I give one more wave and a thank-you to the lady, who just tried to be nice. As I walk down the driveway looking at the frame in the bag, I wonder about my mom. I hope she is a kind person like that. Wherever she is.

Chapter 12

ZONKED!

When I hear the knock on the door, I hope it's Aimee and Michael, but instead I find Brandy and Tressa.

"Hey!" Tressa says. "We thought we'd come by to say hi."

They smile, but the little voice warns me.

I open the door for them, and Tressa scrunches up her tiny, pale face as she enters. Brandy follows.

Grammy is watching one of our favorite game shows, *Let's Make a Deal*, and munching cheese curls.

"Hi, girls." She smiles, waving with orange fingertips. "You're just in time for the big deal." A man dressed as a ketchup bottle is trying to decide between keeping his gold envelope or trading it for curtain number three. I step closer.

Tressa leans forward. "Why is that guy dressed like ketchup?"

Grammy glances at her like she just landed in a spaceship. "*Let's Make a Deal!*"

Tressa looks panicked. "A deal on what?"

Grammy laughs, and Tressa's face darkens.

"*Let's Make a Deal*. It's a game show," I tell her.

The ketchup-bottle guy on TV gets ZONKED! and then there's a commercial. Grammy turns to us. "Well, jeepers crow. I told that man to stick with his gold envelope. But it didn't matter how much I told him, he gave it up anyway. People just never listen." Then she throws up her hands in disgust but puts on a smile. "Hello there, Brandy darlin'. How have you been?"

"I'm fine, Mrs. McHill. How are you?"

"I'm dandy, honey. Just dandy." Then she looks at Tressa. "Who's your new friend?"

"I'm Tressa Bohlen. Nice to meet you."

"Nice to meet you," Grammy says. "I've seen you down at Seaside. Are you staying in one of the cottages?"

"No, my family rented a house on Sea Street."

Grammy drops another cheese curl in her mouth. Then she holds the bag toward us. "You want a nibble?"

"No thank you," Tressa says, like she's caught a whiff of rotten meat.

"Well, you all run along," Grammy says. "I'm goin' to watch the final round here and see if this box of tulips can take home any money." She laughs as she picks up the remote control. "Be a good girl and get me another root beer, will ya, baby?"

Brandy and Tressa follow me into the kitchen. "What's a 'box of tulips'?" Tressa asks.

"That means he looks good but he isn't very smart."

She laughs but not like she thinks it's funny.

I lead them to my room. Tressa draws her finger along the wall, leaving an off-white line. Her fingertip is the color of charcoal. She stares at it.

"That's just the soot from the winter," I tell her.

"Soot?" Her eyes expand.

"Yeah. Something about the furnace. It comes up with the heat or something."

Her mouth moves the slightest bit. Like it's trying to decide what to say.

Tressa wipes the soot from her finger right onto my bedspread.

There is a chirp behind us.

"Birdie!" I call, and run to the cage where my parakeet dances back and forth.

"Hey, Birdie. How have you been?" Brandy asks. She leans in. "Why is his nose black?"

I pause. "I guess it's the soot."

Looking at Birdie, it's the first time I really notice the soot. We all breathe it in, and that can't be good. Tressa asks what time it is—a polite way of saying she has to leave.

"Brandy? You want to hang out?" I ask.

Her eyes dart to Tressa and back to me. "Naw. I think I'll go, too."

Their entire visit lasted less than fifteen minutes.

• • •

The tide has shifted. At least Brandy has.

Grammy's laughter over a big win calls me downstairs, and I plop down on the couch next to her and rest my cheek against her pillowy arm.

She pats my cheek a few times before plunging her hand into her bag of cheese curls. "What's the matter with my girl?"

I sigh. "Nothing."

"Oh, if you say nothing, it's always something. Now spill it for your ole grammy."

I want to say that I am a rock crab and Tressa is a seagull, but I know Grammy would say I am being dramatic.

"I'm just sad, I guess."

"Now, don't let yourself go to the sad place for *too* long. Folks sometimes plop themselves right in the middle of it and get real comfortable."

"Well, it's not like I have a choice."

"Course you do. You gotta make a deal with yourself to *not* do that. You've got to put your arm around happiness and invite it inside." Grammy pauses and looks at me. "But I suspect those girls are making it hard to do that, huh?"

I nod.

"Well, you just push those two out of your head. They don't deserve one more iota of your attention."

But I desperately want things back to the way they were with Brandy.

"And maybe," Grammy continues, "just maybe this isn't as bad as you think. Sometimes people's way of acting has nothing to do with you. You and Brandy have been friends a long time. Maybe if you show her how much her friendship means to you . . ."

"That could be a disaster." And I feel sad because I never used to have to wonder what Brandy would think.

"Well," Grammy says, "you either succeed or you learn. If it doesn't work out, you can handle it. You'll be sad, but you can handle it. That Brandy Fiester won't break my girl."

I manage a smile, but all I can think about is Tressa. It's weird—I don't even like her, but I still wish she liked me.

"Jeepers crow!" Grammy yells, focusing back on the TV. "How'd this boy get on this show, anyway? I've known cockroaches that know more than him!"

"Galveston, Texas," I say, because that was the answer to the last question. Grammy elbows me and giggles.

She looks so proud that I add, "And it wasn't just a storm—it was a category four hurricane with sustained winds of one hundred and forty-five miles per hour."

"Delsie, you surely are the smartest thing on two feet. You could even be a game show champion someday."

"Yeah, me and that bag of cheese curls. I am also packed full of vitamins A and D."

You'd think the walls would come down with Grammy's laughing the way she does. I mean, it wasn't *that* funny. I guess she's laughing mostly because she's my grammy.

Chapter 13

THE RIFT

I run across the grass toward the ocean after Mrs. Fiester tells me that Brandy is down on the beach. I hear them both before I even see them. Their laughter rises above the sand. Along with the sounds of rocks hitting the bottoms of our metal pails.

Brandy and Tressa are collecting rocks and shells in our old pails. My hand hurts from squeezing the railing.

I hear an *oomph* off to the right and lean forward to see around the tall Cape grass.

The boy in black, Ronan, is on the beach, but today his feet are bare and his jeans are soaked to the knee. "Oomph!" he says again as he hurls a rock much farther than I would have figured a person his size could throw.

There is loud laughter again. Brandy and Tressa have seen me, but when I look in their direction, Tressa hits

Brandy on the arm and they both turn toward the water. Their shoulders shake. Laughing again.

Tressa turns back around and leans toward Brandy to say something. By the time I get there, they are quiet.

"Oomph!" *Splash* goes the next rock from the boy.

"Hey!" I say, trying my best to sound like I'm not ready to throw up on their feet. "Whatcha doing?"

"Building a house," Tressa says.

"Out of rocks?" I ask. They wouldn't build a fairy house together, would they?

"Uh . . . I was kidding," Tressa says, half laughing. "We're collecting stuff. Hanging out."

"Can I help?" I ask.

Brandy doesn't say anything, but she hands me her pail, which surprises me.

We collect stuff but don't talk to each other. The beach is starting to fill up. A group of kids comes toward us, laughing and dragging boogie boards, reminding me of better times.

And then there's the boy throwing rocks into the waves. "Oomph!" *Splash*.

"Hey, Delsie," Tressa says. "I think there are some good ones down there. Why don't you check it out?"

"Okay," I say, feeling a little better.

I take about ten steps away, bend over, and pick up a perfect scallop shell. "Brandy! This one is perfect!"

"Cool." Brandy smiles. Tressa watches her.

"No," Tressa says. "Further down."

I take another five steps.

"Keep going," she says, shielding her face from the sun.

I step away again, but I know it won't be enough. She wants me to step all the way to China.

"Yup. Keep going," she calls.

Instead of backing up, I scurry over to Brandy, reach into my pocket, and pull out the rock that I decorated for her. "Here. I made this for you," I tell her. "It's a perfect skipping rock, but I decided to decorate it with glitter like we used to."

"Thanks," Brandy says. She reads the quote I painted on it out loud: "As a friend, on a scale from one to ten, you're a ten and a half." She smiles again, and before she can say anything else, Tressa slaps the bottom of Brandy's hand, sending the rock into the air. Then she catches it and skips it into the ocean. It all happens in a half second.

"Hey!" Brandy says.

"Well, you heard her," Tressa says. "She said it was a great skipping rock."

Don't cry, I tell myself. *Don't.*

But I can't keep the tears from coming. First the sunscreen and now this. And Brandy just stands there like a pile of seaweed. It's like she's a stranger. The idea of not having her as a friend anymore does me in. So I turn to leave. I take two steps.

"Wait! Come back!" Tressa calls.

"Oomph!" *Splash* goes the next rock from the boy.

I don't know why I turn around. Maybe a really dumb part of me thinks they'll be kind if they see me cry, that they'll feel sorry and we can all be friends.

But when I turn around, Tressa is laughing. "Wow. Are you actually *crying*?"

Brandy takes a step toward me and stops, and I know if she has to choose, she won't choose me.

I cry harder. Enough to hear myself, and I hate it. But the sound of Tressa's fake crying in the background of my real crying is even worse. I am humiliated.

"*Hey!*" A loud, deep voice cuts into my own noise. I look up.

It's Ronan. He squeezes a large rock in his hand.

"Leave. Her. *Alone.*"

The two stand silent. Unmoving. We all do.

Then he steps forward and says something I'd have never expected. "I cry sometimes. Don't *you*?"

● ● ●

By the time I get to the house, *Wheel of Fortune* is already on. Grammy eats from a tube of saltine crackers; the crumbs on her chest remind me of the sand I just left.

"Hey there! How's my girl?"

"Fine."

"Good day?"

"Uh-huh."

We sit in silence except for when Grammy leans forward to speak to Spencer from Topeka. "Man alive! How many letters do you need? It's right under your nose!"

Spencer promptly gives the right answer, and Grammy falls back with the satisfaction that she has helped him win a couple grand.

When a commercial comes on, Grammy turns to me. "Something happen to hurt you today, baby?"

I'm not really surprised she knows; Grammy seems to hear me the most when I don't say anything at all.

I want to rest on her soft shoulder, but I know I only have until Spencer comes back from the commercial break. "Brandy and Tressa don't want me around anymore."

"Oh, I'm so sorry. That must hurt something awful."

"Yeah. I gave Brandy a present, and . . . I ended up crying, and they made fun of me."

She gathers me up in her pillowy arm and kisses the top of my head. "Now, there's nothing wrong with crying if you're a human. Lizards and ants and buffalo—they don't cry as far as I know. But if a person can break into laughter, then what's wrong with a few tears?"

I look up at her and shrug.

"Nothin'. Absolutely *nothing*. But there is something you must remember about those feelings deep down inside. They come from your soul, and they're a precious thing.

They should be saved for the ones who'll be cradling them like a new baby. You don't hand them off to just anyone. The ones that love you protect your feelings because they've been given a piece of you. Others may toss them around for just the same reason."

The *Wheel of Fortune* music begins. Grammy reaches for another saltine, and I know that she will have no more to say. I sit unmoving. My eyes watch the game on TV, but I can't tell you if the guy from Topeka loses, wins, or dies. I just know that I'll never forget what she's said to me and I swear I'll never make the same mistake again.

Chapter 14

RETURN OF THE MADRE

Running where the waves touch the beach makes it feel like I'm running faster than I am. My entire body hurts, but I won't slow down. It feels like trying to wring out a towel that just isn't wet enough to drip anymore and yet you keep squeezing and twisting, hoping that some drops will fall.

And I look at a bright blue sky and where it touches the ocean, and I hear a voice tell me that I don't belong anywhere. Not with anyone.

I go from a sprint.

To a run.

To a jog.

To a walk.

To standing still on the beach with the water rolling over my feet.

And wondering what I should do next and remembering that Grammy says you should always follow your heart. But it doesn't seem smart to follow something that is broken.

All of a sudden, the boy in black runs up to me, huffing and puffing. "Finally," Ronan says.

Huh?

"We started running at the same place, but you left me behind back by the jetty where it was like you pushed a turbo button or something. You run like a machine. It's crazy."

"Thanks." I turn to go.

"Can I have a rematch?"

"We weren't racing."

"Well, I guess *you* weren't. But I was until I got a cramp and had to stop."

"Sounds like an excuse."

"Nope, just a fact. So, rematch?"

"Yeah, but not now. I've got to get home. We're having a cookout tonight."

"*Lucky* . . . I wish we were having a cookout."

And without thinking, I turn to him and say, "Well, you can come. Do you want to?" I guess I ask because of the thing he did on the beach—*that* was pretty cool. I want to ask him why he cries. But I don't.

"Really? You're inviting me to a cookout?"

I shrug. "Sure. Why not? You eat, don't you?"

"Whenever possible," he says, smiling. "And a burger? Yeah, I'll come. Your parents don't mind?"

I take a sharp breath in. "No. They won't mind at all."

• • •

We come up the road just in time to hear Henry's old captain's bell signaling that he's ready to start dinner. Henry stands near Olive's enormous pine and brightens when he sees me.

"Hey, Delsie!" He waves. "Your grammy just called to say she'll be late."

We walk toward Henry but have to pass Ruby, who is casting a fishing line up into the trees.

"Uh-oh." I warn Ronan, "Be careful. She may have a lure or hook on that thing."

She whips the pole back over her shoulder, and Ronan dives into the bushes.

"Ruby!" I yell. "Is there a hook on that?"

"No, sorry to scare you," she says. "I'm practicing to work on Daddy's boat!"

"And you're doing a fine job with just a sinker on that line." Henry walks over. "Who's your friend?" he asks.

Ronan steps forward and extends his hand. "Ronan Gale, sir. Nice to meet you."

Henry shakes his hand. "Good handshake there, Ronan.

I respect anyone with a good, firm shake. And it's good to have another guy around. You know, I'm kind of out-numbered here." Then he winks at me. "But of course, I wouldn't have it any other way."

Henry heads over to the half-barrel grill and lights it up.

"I wonder if Olive will show," I say, thinking aloud.

"Who's Olive?"

"Lady that lives in the green house. She promised last time that she wouldn't come to any more neighborhood cookouts right after Henry said he was making a sign for the neighborhood entrance that read WELCOME TO THE DOG HOUSES because the colors of our three houses are the three colors of the things you most often put on hot dogs—red, yellow, and green. Olive stormed off, saying she wouldn't have her home compared to relish, which is nothing but mushed-up pickles, which are nothing but vinegar-soaked cucumbers. Grammy says that some folks just want to be mad about nothing."

He grins. "So a woman named Olive lives in a green house? So who lives in the other houses? Apple and Banana?"

"Yeah." I laugh. "You have a point."

"So, which condiment do you live in?"

"Mustard, but I wish I lived in ketchup."

"Me too!" he says. "I used to try telling my mom it was a vegetable, but she kept saying tomatoes are a fruit, so it would be more like a jelly." Then he points at the abandoned house. "Who lives in the old white one? Is that the hot dog bun?"

"That's a good one—you'll have to tell Henry. But that bun's been empty for a long time."

"It looks it."

I feel Olive's presence before I see her. The same way an animal senses storms and seeks shelter.

"Hello there, Olive!" Henry says. "So glad you could make it!"

Olive does not say hello. "I came out here because someone has to do something about that child casting things around this neighborhood. You know that I love that tree. You know that, Henry. Goodness knows what she'll do to it."

"Speaking of the weather . . ." he begins, and laughs at Olive's expression.

"Don't you go changing the subject on me again, Henry Isaac Lasko."

Henry puts his arm around Olive's shoulders. "Now, that child can't do a thing to that enormous tree. You know that."

"Humpft." Then Olive looks over at Ronan. "If you're planning on robbing my house, I'll save you the trouble. I've got nothing worth stealing."

"What?" I blurt out. "Why would you *say* that? You

don't even *know* him." Sometimes Olive makes me feel like a category five storm.

"Why, just look at him—he's dressed like a hooligan," she says.

Henry shakes his head. He motions to Ronan to ignore her.

Olive straightens and points at Ruby. "And she threw a rock at my house."

"She did no such thing," Henry says, but I can tell by the way Ruby shrinks that she did do it. And when Henry looks at her, he knows, too.

"*Ruby Loren*," he says.

"I was trying to hit the tree. And I missed. So does that count if it was by accident?"

"It certainly does count!" Olive snaps. "My goodness, child. You wouldn't know how to walk in a two-person parade."

"Olive. *Tinselly!*" Henry says. He moves closer to his daughter and gives her a hug. "Ruby is a good girl. Don't say otherwise."

"Why is she so mean?" Ronan tries to whisper, but it comes out loud enough for everyone to hear.

Olive stands there like she's trying to answer the question for herself. Her face looks like something hurts deep inside, and I swear that I hear her mumble that she's sorry. I can scarcely believe it.

The sound of a car coming up the road makes us all turn. It's bright yellow. A taxi.

I can't remember a single taxi coming to visit us ever in my life.

I run to it. Something deep inside tells me this is something good, and as I get closer, the car stops and a purple suede high-heeled shoe hits the ground, and I know I'm right about it being good news.

"Esme!" I yell. "You're *home!*"

"Sugar pop!" she calls.

Henry and Ruby are there in a flash.

Henry picks Esme up and swings her around while Ruby jumps up and down nearby. It's only a second before Esme reaches out and draws her in like she's pulling her into a life raft. And it must feel that way to Ruby. The way she goes from moving to standing to going all gooey and pressing herself against the two of them.

Esme turns and reaches for me. "Delsie! What are you *waiting* for? Come on *over* here!" She reaches for me, and I join the group of them. I feel complete. The neighborhood is whole again.

Chapter 15

THAT NOURISHING TEA

The next day, Esme invites me over. "Shall I put on some tea?" she asks as we walk into her kitchen. I stare up at the MAY THE FISH BE WITH YOU sign over the sink that I made for Henry after we watched *Star Wars*.

It's a hot day, so Esme prepares iced tea. Reaching into the cupboard, she pulls out the Strong Shoulder mason jars. She smiles at me as she works and I feel all warm inside because I just love Esme so much.

Ruby trips on a stool as she crashes into the room. She tries to sit in a chair but misses it the first time she tries. Sometimes that girl is like a walking wrecking ball.

The front door opens and Henry comes in. Ruby charges him. "Daddy! Did you catch me a fish today?"

"Ruby! I caught you a whole box of fish sticks. How's that?"

"Oh, Daaaddy . . ."

"There they were. A box of 'em just floating there in the water." He laughs and kisses her on the head before reaching into the cabinet for a glass.

Esme comes over and kisses him on the cheek. "Bad jokes mean bad fishing?"

"Yeah . . . Other crews were reporting over the radio that the fish were biting at everything from bran muffins to belt buckles. But not us."

"Daddy! Fish don't eat *belt* buckles."

He laughs. "They don't? No wonder I didn't catch a lot today."

"So how tough was it?" Esme asks.

"Not the best but we've been doing real good lately, so . . ." He turns to me. "Hey there, Delsie. When are you going to come on the boat with me and spread some of that McHill fishing luck around?"

I sit straighter. "I'll come if you ask me."

He leans forward. "Well, I'm askin'!" he says. He's laughing, but I can see the worry swooshing around inside of him. Looking up at the Massachusetts license plates on the mantel—ones from 1928 and 1929—I'm reminded of how superstitious the local fishermen are. When there were no fish in '28, they blamed it on the new design of the license plate. The next year they demanded it be fixed—and the fish returned. I guess all fishermen worry about one bad day rolling into a whole bunch of them.

"I'm betting, Delsie McHill," he says, opening the fridge and grabbing a bunch of grapes, "that you have that fish-whispering gift just like Papa Joseph and your mom, Mellie."

I look up so fast, I nearly spill my tea. "My mom liked to fish?"

"Oh yeah. And she was good at it, too. A lot of people think fishing is about luck. It isn't. It's about instincts, and your mom sure had good ones.

"You know, there's the basics of finding fish. The fish like the rips. Or changes in the tide. If seagulls are circling or dive-bombing an area, there are fish. Head out to sea before the sun is too high in the sky, because once the sun is up, the striper dive; they like the cooler water. But it was like Mellie could just sniff out the fish. Your grandfather used to joke if she'd just sit on the bow of the boat, he'd only have to fish half the time."

I am shocked. How come I didn't know this?

He taps my nose. "I thought I'd tell you that, since your grammy told me you've been wondering about your mom."

Henry spins away and scoops up Ruby. "How's my girl?" he asks. "You want to go outside and play some Whiffle Ball with your old man before supper?" And they are out the door before she can even answer. Of course, it was a *yes*. Ruby loves to hit things. Although she misses a lot.

I look down at my Strong Shoulder jar, and I don't feel

strong at all. I miss Brandy. And I long for my mother. How can you long for someone you don't even know?

"Sooo?" Esme asks, drawing out the word. Her voice is soft. I think I must look goofy, like I want to cry.

"Can I ask you a question?" I ask.

She leans forward on her elbow. "Of course. Anything."

And all of a sudden, the question runs from me. Or the courage to ask it does. I sip some tea, trying to come up with a different question that doesn't have to do with the reasons a mother would leave. Or wouldn't stay.

"You always call your tea 'that nourishing tea,' but it's nothing but water and a bunch of dried leaves. That doesn't seem nourishing to me."

Esme throws her head back and laughs. "You know, that's a very fair question, and I feel silly for never having explained it to you, sugar pop."

"Explained what?"

"'That nourishing tea' is something my mother used to call it. I asked her a similar question when I was about your age, and she told me something I've never forgotten. When people are sad about things. Or lonely. Or angry. Or confused. Or any of the emotions that we people would rather avoid, they sometimes try to chase those feelings away with the wrong things. But a good cup of tea can make us feel so much better."

"Wow, your mom really liked tea."

She laughs a bit. "It *isn't* the tea, Delsie. It's that tea is so often shared. That's when friends lean forward and look each other in the eye. They laugh. They do more than hear; they *listen*. They *connect*, and anything that matters in this *whole* . . . *wide* . . . *world* is about connection. It's what makes all the hard stuff I talk about bearable."

I nod.

She leans forward and places her hand on my arm. "Visiting with good friends like you, Delsie."

I know that's supposed to make me happy and I should agree, but I can't get what's caught in my throat unstuck.

I stand up. "I have to go. Grammy is probably wondering where I am."

Her face questions me.

There's so much I can't say. I can't tell her how Madre Seal coming back makes me curl up and pull the covers under my chin at night. I can't tell her one of my best friends has chosen a new best friend. And I can't tell Esme that I don't want her to be my friend; I want her and Henry to be my mom and dad. I'm glad they love me, but it feels like having the light of the sun but not its warmth.

• • •

It's been cloudy all day. Now when I step outside, rain begins to hit the ground like missiles. But nothing is going to stop me from training for the 5K run.

I do a few stretches to warm up, thinking about the

clouds. How they get darker and darker as they collect more water molecules inside of them. Then when the moisture gets to be too much, and the cloud gets too heavy, they fall to earth as rain. I feel like that lately. Heavy. Like everything is building up and will end in some kind of storm.

I study the abandoned house across from us. I wonder why the people left it behind. Did they figure out it wasn't a good house? Did they find a better one? Do they ever think about it now?

I begin my run. Hoping I can outrun being so lonely.

The rain comes so hard, the earth can't soak it up. Swift rivers of it run along the curbs. Gutters become waterfalls. Puddles send water up my legs as my feet crash into the middle of them. The thing about the rain is that you can't stop it. It needs to find places to go. Our basement is made with thick walls of concrete, but I know after a storm like this there will be water.

And when the storm finally passes and the sun comes out, the water will evaporate and leave everything dry again. But you know that the rain will eventually return. Because that is what rain does.

Things that I'd rather not think about remind me of the rain. The thoughts seep into everything. They rise and overflow. They may recede for a while, but they always return.

Chapter 16

A BOWL OF BOLOGNA

I come home with a pile of pictures taken with my new camera and start the "Wall of the Left Behind" in my bedroom. I put up the picture of the abandoned house in my neighborhood. Then the pictures of towels on benches, deserted cars, and lost jackets. A sneaker, a baby stroller, and a T-shirt. I'm surprised how many things people leave behind. I wonder if they miss them later.

The house is filled with smoke when I come downstairs. Which means that Grammy is making fried bologna for dinner. Turns out that when you fry a piece of bologna in butter, it goes from a flat piece to a bowl shape. Grammy never gets tired of it. She thinks it's some kind of miracle. Then she fills hers with mustard. Lots and lots of bright yellow mustard.

Ronan is coming over for dinner, and I wonder what he'll think of this.

He arrives just in time. He has a Portuguese tart from his dad's favorite bakery to share with us. Grammy is so excited, you'd think she won the Showcase Showdown.

We sit right away. Grammy leans over and pats Ronan on the shoulder. "Well, Ronan. Thank you for coming over to share our meal with us. It isn't fancy, but it's a favorite around here."

"That's okay," he says. "I'm not that fancy. In case you didn't notice."

Grammy laughs loud as she scoops a heaping glob of yellow mustard into her bologna bowl. Then another blob. And another.

Ronan watches but doesn't seem to react. Then he scoops out a blob of mustard. And another. And another. And then unscrews the top of the pepper and pours some of that on top. It's almost like they're competing to see whose mouth will catch on fire first. I wonder if we have a fire extinguisher.

Ronan eats more fried bologna than is natural. He eats it up like it's the best thing ever, and I wonder what his father makes for dinner.

After Grammy and Ronan finish off the jar of mustard, I stand to clear the dishes, and Ronan gets up to help.

"You're a fine guest to help out like that, Ronan," Grammy says. "Your parents have done a fine job."

I think he means to say thanks, but it almost seems like he doesn't know how.

When Ronan asks for a dish towel to dry the dishes, Grammy laughs. "No need for that, now. We let God dry the dishes here." She lumbers toward the TV. "Well," she says, "it's time for some *Family Feud*."

"Seems like a funny thing to wish for," Ronan says.

"You're a funny one, you know that?" She settles into her couch and turns to Ronan again. "Your dad must be waiting on you. You need to head home soon?"

"Naw," he says. Then he turns to me. "Want to play Monopoly?"

"Our first game took about four hours."

"So? You won, didn't you? I mean barely, but you won."

"Barely? I don't think so. I wiped the board with you."

He smirks. "Yeah, whatever. You want to play or not?"

We set up the homemade Monopoly game that my mother made out of paper when she was my age. The board is the real one that she found at a tag sale with Grammy for only five cents, so she decided to take it and make the rest— the cards, the money, and the deeds. Everything but the tokens. We use old coins that Papa found on the beach with his metal detector for those. I choose the buffalo nickel. Ronan chooses the bicentennial silver dollar.

Whenever I use this game, I think about what it would

have been like to play it with my mother. I bet we would have been friends if we were the same age.

Ronan gets lucky, getting all of the yellows and greens pretty fast. But I end up with a bunch of the cheaper properties, so we trade money back and forth. The game lasts forever. When we're finally done, Grammy is asleep on the couch.

I shake her shoulder a bit. "Grammy? Grammy? Wake up."

She moans and opens her eyes, looks about, and gets her bearings. "Oh, I fell asleep. What time is it?"

"Midnight. Ronan needs a ride home. Or should he walk?"

"Oh no! I fell asleep! His father must be worried sick. Did you call him?"

"Yeah, I did," Ronan lies. "He says it's okay."

I look at him, but he won't look back.

Grammy stands up. "Well, I'll freshen up a bit and then we'll go. You two wait outside, but don't go disappearing on me."

We head outside. "So," I ask, "why did you tell Grammy that you called your dad?"

He puts his hands in his pockets and walks in a small circle. "I don't know."

I know he does.

"I didn't want your grammy to worry or be mad at me. And it makes no difference if I call my father or not. I can walk in at any time."

Having no curfew sounds good.

And then I begin to wonder if that's true.

Chapter 17

ESCAPE FROM THE CAKES

I've just let Ronan in when Grammy calls from the kitchen, "Delsie, honey bunch! I've got some chicken legs that are past due if you want them!"

"Really?! *Ex*cellent."

Ronan looks at me like I've lost my mind. "Why the heck would anyone want old chicken?"

I shake my head. "The things you don't know about living on the Cape."

"Well, if it involves old chicken legs, I think I can wait."

"You'll see," I say. "You're going to love it."

"Oh yeah. Nothing like rotting meat to improve the day."

●●●

When we arrive at Gray's Beach, I open my bag and pull out the chicken, some string, and scissors. "Here," I say, handing him the scissors. "We need long pieces of string."

He cuts the string, glancing at me. As I tie the string tightly around the chicken leg, Ronan looks over the side of the boardwalk. "So we're here to catch stuff?"

"Blue crabs."

"I see one!" he yells as he points. "And another one!" He glances at me, glowing. "They're everywhere!"

I give him a chicken leg, and I take one. We lower the chicken legs over the side and into the water. Mine lies on the bottom, but Ronan's is hanging in a deeper spot.

I lean over. "It has to sit on the bottom somewhere so the crabs can get to it."

He looks over at mine and smiles. The crabs are running from all directions and climbing onto my chicken leg.

"Pull it up!" Ronan says, leaning over the railing.

"Okay. Here's the thing," I say. "Once they are eating, you have to pull them up smoothly but really fast before they fall off. Because they do let go. *Ready?*"

"Yeah." He steps up another rung on the railing.

Hand over hand, just like pulling in nets on the *Reel*, I pull up my string. Two feet over the water, a crab lets go. Then another. When the chicken reaches the railing, I have four crabs left. I lift the string over the railing and drop the chicken into the pail. I knock the crabs off with my hand and pull the chicken out for another round.

Bending over, I say, "Wow. One of them is *huge*. Usually, you can't catch those. Henry says it's a Darwin thing.

They're big because they've figured out how to survive. Like, if you're suddenly being lifted into the air, *let go*."

Ronan reaches into the pail and pulls out the big one. "We should name him Zeus!"

"You can't name things we are taking home to eat."

"Eat? Who wants to eat this? He looks like a mini alien." The crab pinches his finger.

"Ow!" he yells, dropping the crab on the boardwalk.

"It must have heard you."

The crab moves sideways, running for the edge, but hits Ronan's foot. He jumps into the air and falls down flat.

I pick it up from the back so its claws can't reach my hand. It grabs ahold of the edge of the plank, but I pull it off.

"How'd you do that?" he asks.

I turn my hand and show him. "They can't reach you . . . well, most of the time. Sometimes a big, smart one will figure it out and reach under themselves and getcha."

Just then, I get pinched and drop the crab, which makes another run for it.

Ronan laughs. Hard.

"Really?" I ask, going for the crab again. "You're laughing at *me*? You're still lying on the deck after being taken down by something the size of a pancake."

Ronan stands. "I wasn't taken down. I was just resting."

Then he reaches out to take the crab from me. He turns

the crab toward his own face, looks it in the eye, and smiles. "He bubbles."

"Yeah, they do that to keep oxygen moving through their gills," I tell him. "Now put it back in the bucket. Grammy will make some great crab cakes out of it. With extra tartar sauce. You'll love them."

He looks at me. "*Really?* She'll make *crab* cakes?"

"Yeah, she sure will."

He stares down at the crab. And then he lifts the crab and holds it about six inches in front of his face. "He doesn't look tasty."

"Wait until you see him with buttered bread crumbs."

His mouth swings to the side a bit. Then he looks the bubbling crab in the eyes and says, "I dub you with the name Darwin. And now you *owe* me one, Darwin."

He winds up his arm and throws the crab well beyond the reach of chicken on string. It lands with a splash in the marsh.

He tries to hide his smile but doesn't do a great job of it.

"*Wait. What?* Why would you do that?"

He shrugs and smiles bigger. "Sorry. He was beautiful and just such a good fighter. I had to let him go."

"It's okay. That was better than eating crab cakes any day," I say, thinking about how much Papa Joseph would have liked him. He would have said Ronan is a good soul, and I would have to agree.

Chapter 18

WHO WATCHES YOU WHILE YOU EAT A SANDWICH?

I'm so happy when Brandy calls me to ask if I want to come for lunch that I have to keep myself from cartwheeling into a wall. But with every bubble of happiness that rises inside, the little voice taps me on the shoulder.

When I arrive at Seaside, I run into Ronan. "Hey," he says.

I see Brandy and Tressa sitting down near the water at the picnic table already.

"Hey," I say. "How're you doing?"

He looks back over his shoulder. "Better than you, I think."

"What do you mean by that?"

He shrugs. "Nothin'." He pulls some gum out of his pocket. "You want some?"

"No, thanks. I'm going to have lunch with Brandy and Tressa."

"*Why?*"

"Because they asked. And they're my friends."

"They *are?*"

I look past him again. Tressa is looking in my direction. Smiling. "Yeah, they are."

"Hey," he says. "I'd love to eat with a couple of bull sharks. Or maybe they're more like oceanic whitetip sharks. Haven't decided yet." He looks up, thinking. "I don't know. I guess Brandy would be a bull shark. They can go back and forth between salt water and fresh water."

"They're not that bad," I say, getting annoyed.

"*Not that bad* is not something you find in the traits of a friend handbook." He pops a piece of gum into his mouth. "Suit yourself. I just think that there's more to having friends than sitting around a table and letting them watch you eat a sandwich."

I open my mouth to shoot back an answer, but nothing comes out.

He tucks the foil wrapper in his pocket. "Just saying." He shrugs. "Well, see ya."

I watch Ronan walk away for longer than I should. Not so eager for lunch anymore.

"Hey," I say, approaching the picnic table, noticing my feet feel like bricks.

"Hey," Brandy says, and moves over to make room.

Tressa smiles like a cat watching a mouse ease out of its hole. "Thanks for inviting me."

"Her mother made her," Tressa says. Brandy turns red.

They begin to unpack their lunches, which are both in the same cooler with a sea turtle on it. I look down at my brown paper bag. I pull out my root beer and pop it open. As I look at their fancy chicken wraps, I decide that I don't feel like eating a fried bologna sandwich in front of these two.

"That was a blast last night," Tressa says. "Watching the fireworks from the beach was the best."

"Yeah, it was pretty cool," Brandy says. "Every town does theirs on different nights all summer long. So you can always find them somewhere."

Tressa turns to me. "Did you see them?"

"Oh . . . yeah . . . of course we did." Thinking that answering Tressa's questions feels like when the school nurse went through my hair looking for lice in the first grade.

Brandy stares. She knows we don't do stuff like that.

"And then," Tressa continues, "we went to that fire pit pizza place out on the beach. So cool. Have you been there?" she asks.

I hate pizza. Probably the only kid in the world. But I've never liked it. Brandy knows this, and yet I can't help myself. I look at Tressa. "Yeah, who doesn't love that place? We go there all the time."

Now Brandy's head falls to the side, and she gives me a funny look.

"But the coolest thing was the sleepover," Tressa adds. "I can't believe we stayed up until four o'clock in the morning watching that movie. Your mom is cool."

"What movie?" I ask.

Brandy begins to answer, but Tressa cuts in. Like my question is inconvenient. "*Big*. It's an old movie about a kid that wishes to be grown-up and gets his wish from some fortune-teller machine. It was pretty good."

"I saw a good movie on TV. It was about this girl who—"

Tressa interrupts, holding up her hand like she is stopping traffic. "Could you go get more napkins? Inside. Pleeease . . . ?"

I catch Brandy stifling a laugh.

I don't get the napkins as I'm ordered to do because it would be humiliating. Then again, staying is humiliating, too. They talk about other things they've been doing. Things without me. I try to join in one more time, but Tressa talks over me until I give up.

When I stand and say I have to go, they finally get quiet.

As I walk away, my stomach feels awful, which is weird because I didn't even eat anything.

The bubble of happiness I had for this lunch pops like bubbles do. Instantly and completely.

Chapter 19

IS THAT YOU?

"Let's play tourist today," I say to Ronan. "Have you been to Holiday Hill yet?"

"That place with the golf and stuff?" Ronan asks.

I nod.

"I wanted to go, but my dad says he's tired at night. Why? Do you have money?"

"Yeah, I do. When I help Grammy clean rooms, she splits the tip with me. And I also have a bunch of free game coupons that we found in a room after the people left. So between the two, we should be good."

"I don't have any money, though."

"That's okay. It will be worth it to kick your butt at golf."

"You think so, huh? You're a dreamer, Delsie. A dreamer."

We run across Route 28 and straight into the arcade to pay for mini golf. I choose the blue golf ball, and Ronan chooses the green.

On the third hole, I make a hole in one and brag more than I should. I'm happy that I'm doing well at golf, but I'm mostly happy that I don't feel nervous to be around Ronan. I don't have to think about everything I say and do and then worry he won't like it. I don't have to lie about who I am.

On the fifth hole, Ronan is leaping around singing some song about being the champion. He must have made it up, because it's terrible.

"It's only the fifth hole. You haven't won yet. And I'm actually *ahead* of you!"

"I envision myself accepting the trophy. I will be . . ."

And he goes on, but I don't hear a thing. All I can see is a woman with two kids who are much younger than me. Her hair is frizzy and looks like the kind of hair that gets reddish in the summer—just like mine. And she has a cleft chin and blue eyes, just like me.

She looks like the woman in my old candy frame—as if she stepped out of it and into the world. It looks just like her. *Just* like her.

I stuff my hands in my pockets and straighten my back.

Ronan is in front of me. "I'm sorry about bragging so much. It's okay, Delsie. I'll spot you some points."

I shake my head.

"No, it's okay."

"I would never get mad about mini golf." I look around him. "It's that lady." I swallow. "I think she's my mom."

Ronan turns and looks at her. "You think so? Are those her kids?"

"I . . . don't know. We haven't heard from her in a long, long time. I mean . . . I *guess* they could be her kids."

"But you don't know that she's your mom, right? Just a guess?"

"I feel like she is. She looks just like her picture. And . . ." The words catch in my throat. "She looks just like me." I swallow again, hard. "Should I go talk to her?"

"Sure. Because if you don't, you'll regret it."

Ronan is good at cutting to the truth.

Looking down at my golf ball, I get an idea. I toss the ball into the bushes near her. And then I run over.

And standing in front of her makes my stomach roll over and over. I lock eyes with her and watch to see if she recognizes me. How could someone not recognize her own baby?

"Hello," she says.

"Hi. Oh. Sorry. I just came to get my ball." I bend over and reach into the bushes to get it, and when I stand back up, I lock eyes with her again. Hoping for an answer in her face.

"May I help you? Do you need something?" she asks, and the sound of her voice is like Esme's—all sweet and let-me-help-you. I look at her kids and wonder if I have two sisters.

"Are you my momma?" I ask.

One eye squints. "Pardon me?"

"Are you my momma? Is it you?" I squeak like a little kid.

Her lips press together and her eyes get sad and she shakes her head a bit. "Oh, honey. I'm sorry. I'm not your momma. I have these two girls but haven't had any other children besides them." By this time, her two girls are staring at me like I am trying to steal their favorite thing.

"Are you sure?" I ask, starting to cry. "Because you look just like the picture, and you look just like me. Or I look like you . . . so I thought that maybe . . . I thought you could be . . ."

"I'm not. Really. I'm very sorry. But whoever is your mom, she is very lucky."

"Very lucky," I mumble. "Very *lucky*." I drop my golf club and run. I run so fast that Ronan hasn't got a chance of catching me.

• • •

I find myself standing in front of Aimee's. Because it's Saturday, I'm sure she has no rehearsal. I knock on the door.

Aimee swings the door open. "Hey, Dels." Then she gets serious. "Wow. You look like you need water. You want water?"

I nod furiously.

"Come on in."

"No. I have to talk to you. Outside."

She looks worried. "Okay."

When she comes back out with my water, I stop thinking about how to say it and just start talking. "You know how at every open house at school, when the teacher meets your mom, they tell her, 'Oh! Your daughter looks just like you. She's your Mini-Me.' And you smile because your mom is pretty great?"

"Yeah . . ."

"And you know how every spring you complain because you have to wear a dress and go to the father-daughter dance? But you always have fun?"

"Yeah . . ."

"You know how you wanted to know what it's like to be an orphan? For *real*?"

"I'm sorry, Dels. I shouldn't have asked that. I was just so excited—"

"It's okay, Aims. I'm not mad at you. I just didn't know how to answer, that's all. But that's the answer. Never in my life will I go to a father-daughter dance. And no one will ever call me their daughter, and I'll never get to call anyone Mom. That's what it's like."

My hands curl into fists and my voice cracks as I feel the anger hit me like a giant swell in the water. I try to hold it all, but I think I'm doing a terrible job of it.

Even so, Aimee stands shoulder to shoulder with me. "Gee, Dels. That 'Tomorrow' song probably doesn't cut it, huh? 'The sun will come out tomorrow' and 'bet your bottom dollar' and all that. It's terrible, isn't it? I mean, really terrible."

And we laugh. And it makes me feel so much better.

Chapter 20

SEEDS THAT GROW
AND SEEDS THAT DON'T

I talk to Ronan on the phone and tell him I'm okay. He says he can come over for a Monopoly game, but I say maybe tomorrow. Instead, I share popcorn with Grammy on the couch and watch the Game Show Network. We like seeing happy people win things.

It's raining the next morning, and when I wake, I stay in bed and try to hold on to a dream I had of Papa Joseph. We were out searching for old coins with his metal detector.

One of our favorite things to do after a storm was to head to the beach to see what we could find, because a hard rain helps the metal detector pick up signals. We'd see other "detectors" down there, but Papa knew that searching along the walls after a storm was a good way to find things. We found lots of coins—mostly new money but also some buffalo nickels and a silver dollar from the bicentennial.

Papa also loved to go to wooded areas around Concord and Lexington. We found some pieces of metal that could have been musket balls from the Revolutionary War. He was so excited. But he wouldn't take them to a dealer. I think he was afraid he'd find out they weren't anything and he'd rather just keep them and hope.

Out in those fields, he used to talk about finding the mother lode, though: a mason jar of old money. Before the banks were reliable, people used to stuff their belongings in jars and then bury them in the yard. A way to keep locations of valuables secret.

In the kitchen, I pour Cheerios into a bowl, remembering how Papa told me they were donut seeds. What a dumb kid I must have been to spend hours burying them around our yard, waiting for them to sprout.

Grammy shuffles into the kitchen. "Morning, Delsie girl. How about some crooks and nannies?"

"Sure." I laugh. The English muffin box says they have nooks and crannies, but "crooks and nannies" is one of our favorite jokes.

I tell her about my dream. She shakes her head.

"Oh, that silly metal detector of his. Naming it Homer and talking like it was a family member. 'Should we take Homer to the beach with us? Maybe Homer would like to go for a ride.'"

"You call *him* silly? Don't you call your car *Darlin'* every morning?"

She laughs. "I suppose I do. That Darlin' and Homer would make a lovely couple, don't you think?"

"Homer could say he looked for Darlin' his whole life."

I expect her to laugh at my joke, but she looks sad. Shaking her head, she begins to make tea. "Oh, how I miss that man," she tells me. "Remember how happy he'd be on stormy Sunday nights in the summer?"

"Yes! He'd call them Treasure Trove Mondays because tourists had been dropping things on the beach all weekend. Remember the diamond ring?" I ask her. "He actually danced on Corporation Beach."

"Yes, he did. And then he found that sign for a lost ring— oh, that girl was so happy to get it back!"

I smile thinking about going with him to meet the girl. Watching a complete stranger throw her arms around Papa Joseph. It was also the first time I saw anyone cry—really cry—from being just plain happy.

"I've been thinking about Papa's treasures, actually," Grammy says. "Those half-cent coins he found in Concord must be worth something, and his pocket watch would be worth a lot. It might be time to visit the dealer again." She sighs.

"*Grammy*. We can't sell Papa's *things*."

"Delsie, I *know*. I *do*. But the watch alone would fix all of the problems with that car. And that old furnace. It may be hot today, but the wind will howl on the Cape before we know it. We'll need heat. *Without* soot."

"I'd rather be cold."

Her shoulders droop. "To be honest, Delsie, having his stuff around just stirs things up for me—reminds me of what I've lost." Then she comes over and places her hand on my face. "Thank the lord I have you."

"But, Grammy—"

"Baby, we *need* the money. And now Henry tells me the roof will need work, too."

She looks weary.

I know she's right. About the money. But I feel differently about things.

Thinking back to our metal-detecting days, I get an idea of how to keep Papa's stuff safe. And I know that it's wrong, but the need to hold on to the little pieces I have left of the people I love is overwhelming.

Once Grammy leaves for work, I run up the stairs and get the Strong Shoulder jar I got at the tag sale and unscrew the top. I line it with toilet paper to make a cushion on the bottom.

I go into Papa's drawer and pick up the box where he kept his treasures. He called them memory shakers—things that reminded him of good times.

I go through the box and find Papa's sterling silver pocket watch and rub the figure of the fisherman standing in a rowboat. He's got an Irish cap just like Papa wore. The chain attached swings back and forth. I push the button, and the lid pops open. It's still running. I swallow hard, thinking of the millions of times he opened that watch to check the tides. Gently, I place the watch in the jar.

I search the box for more treasures and find the round pieces of white metal that Papa thought were musket balls and two British half cents from Concord.

There is a pirate's coin from Pirate's Cove, the big mini golf place on 28. I'm pretty sure this is mine, so I slip it in my pocket. I smile, thinking this memory shaker must be about me.

There are some pins from General Electric because Papa's father worked there with Olive's father. They were friends, so Papa knew Olive his whole life.

There is a Strong Shoulder mason jar, but it's only about three inches tall. Not much use for drinking tea. Jelly maybe? Except the lid has a slot in it. I think it's a bank for coins.

A key chain that says DATSUN on it. I wonder what that is. I try to think if I've ever heard of Datsun, Massachusetts.

There are two little discs about the size of checkers. One says THE WHALE, and one says THE SHIP. I love them. They have ridges on the side like quarters do.

There is a scrimshaw knife with an etching of a great white and a message in a bottle in its stomach on it. I wonder where he got it. I wish I could ask him.

I find the lures that Papa made from old spoons and pieces of wood. I recognize the multicolored fish with the crooked eye. It was his first lure. He used to say, "This was the beginning of my acquisition of great wealth." And then he'd lean back, laughing. He'd pull me close. He'd kiss the top of my head and say, "I don't have a lot of digits in my bank account, but I'm a wealthy man indeed."

Grammy is right. Holding his things makes me ache with the missing of him—and I understand what she meant about being sad when she sees them. But I feel *more* than that—the memories make me happy, too. I like thinking about him, and I'm happy that he was my papa. The happy and sad are like two hands clasped together. I wish I could share these feelings with Grammy.

I add Papa's knife and the coins to the jar, and when I go to put the box back in his dresser, I find another box. Wondering what it is, I slide it out. Written on top, in Grammy's swirly handwriting, is *My Mellie*. I gasp a bit and slowly lift the lid, feeling like she might step out of it.

There is a necklace made of tiny stones in all different

colors. It's so beautiful that I wonder why she didn't take it with her. But then there are lots of things she should have taken with her.

I'm surprised to find a ticket from a Mariah Carey concert. My mom wrote *We Belong Together* in blue pen across the top. I wonder who she was thinking about when she wrote that.

And there are two rings—the first is a small ring with a little stone on top. It's beautiful. I slip it on my finger and admire it. I'd like to keep it, but Grammy would see. It can't be a diamond. If there were any diamonds around here, I'd know it.

The other ring has a whale that wraps around your finger. I love it, too.

There's a collection of root beer bottle caps. I guess she did like root beer like Grammy and me.

I place her things in the jar and fill the rest of it with toilet paper and screw on the lid extra tight. Then I carry it out to Papa's shed and find his shovel. I find a patch with as few dandelions as I can and skim the grass with the shovel, carefully removing a sheet of dirt and sand and grass. Then I start digging the hole.

When it's finished, I hold the jar one last time. I look down at the things Papa loved, and the hole he's left by being gone feels so deep and wide, I can't find a way up and out. I remember how he always smelled like coffee and he leaned forward and listened to every word when I told him a story. Missing him makes me sad . . . but at least there are lots of good memories, too. With my mom it is different—having to wonder what I've missed with her is a whole other kind of empty.

I place the jar in the hole and fill in around the edges with dirt. Then I cover the rest and replace the patch of long grass and dandelions.

Walking back to the shed, I notice Henry has his snow shovel out. It's leaning against the front of the house like it does every summer—a reminder of colder, harsher times. He says it's good to remember the hard times in the middle of the good ones. Never take anything for granted.

Before Papa died, I thought that was dumb. Not anymore.

Chapter 21

NOT-SO-PERFECT PICTURE

I come back from the drugstore with more prints for the Wall of the Left Behind.

As I tape them up, though, I hesitate. Why a wall of abandoned objects? Am I supposed to understand how a towel feels about being left on a bench? I mean, I guess I'm trying to be deep, but maybe it's just dumb. So I think that I should add some regular family pictures, too.

I go to Grammy's closet and pull down the picture album. Tucked into the pages, I see my report card from last year when the teacher wrote I have potential. I got in trouble for telling her I thought that was just a nice way of calling me a failure. But Grammy says it's a compliment and that potential is like coupons in a drawer; if you leave them there, they are nothing but scraps of paper.

The pictures on the first few pages make me smile. And I wish that Grammy were the type to put pictures in frames and hang them up.

I grab the loose Halloween picture of Esme dressed in waders, holding a fishing pole, and Henry dressed as a giant fish. This was last year, and I remember him saying over and over that he was the catch of her life. She both agreed and rolled her eyes at him.

There are lots of birthday pictures, and I smile at all the lopsided cakes. It's been a joke with Grammy that, no matter how hard she tries, her cakes are always crooked. She says love isn't perfect and so why should a cake filled with love be? One of these will cheer my wall up.

Then I spot an older picture—I look past the cake and me ready to blow out the candles. I'm still smiling when I notice her. The woman standing behind me in the picture.

It's the woman from the candy frame.

It's my mother.

She was *there*.

My fingertips turn white as I hold the picture. I stare, feeling sick and happy all at the same time. Blinking. Is it really *her*?

The door closes downstairs, and Grammy calls to me, "Delsie girl! I'm home!"

Home.

By the time I reach the bottom of the stairs, my chest hurts. I cannot get the air out of my lungs in order to fill them again.

Grammy is in the kitchen, and I stand in the doorway. "Whew! What a day. I think I'll smell like Pine-Sol right up until the day I meet my maker."

Whenever I have had a question for Grammy, a heart question—the kind of question that Esme would ask over tea—we've been on the couch, snuggled up together.

So it feels strange to be standing so far away. *Waiting*. Waiting for the courage to ask the question—or hear the answer.

"I have to ask you something," I blurt out.

"*Any*thing, Delsie. You know *that*."

"I need the truth. You *prom*ise?"

She looks concerned. "I never lie to you. I don't have to."

"Did my mother come back? Come home? When I was little?"

She sees the picture at my side and takes a deep breath. "She did," she says, sounding ready to wrap me up in her arms. Like when I was little and scraped my knees. "She showed up on your third birthday. We didn't even know that she was coming."

"And then she left again?"

She nods.

I try to swallow the lump in my throat. "So she left me *twice*, then?"

"Yes, she did . . . but—"

"Why didn't you make her staaaay?" I interrupt. The sound of the last word, the way I draw out the vowel, makes me hear how much I wanted that.

"She left because . . . well . . . because . . ."

"Just *tell* me, please."

I know my grammy. She is standing there trying to think of a way to soften the news. Of how my mother wanted to leave again and she and Papa begged her to stay but she wouldn't. I know she's trying to be kind, but it begins to walk up my back, and I snap, "*Grammy!*"

She steps forward. "She wasn't ready to be your momma."

"What do you mean? She thought it was too much trouble? Like, too much work or something?"

"No." Grammy begins to tear up, making her eyes look bluer. "She . . . Well, Delsie. The truth . . . the *truth* . . . is that I made her go."

It's like she speaks a foreign language. I don't understand. "Wh-what? You *made* her go? She wanted to stay?"

She nods. "Well, it was a long time ago now," she tells me. "And the problem was that she was doing things a person just shouldn't be doing when they are taking care of a child. I told her over and over that anytime she wanted

115

to quit those things and be the mother you needed, she was welcome back."

I pace when I want to sprint.

This whole thing feels like the world has flipped upside down and I'm dangling, just trying to hold on. I make a sound like a puppy who's been stepped on.

"It's okay," she whispers.

"It's *not* okay!" I say even louder than I expected. "How could you *do* that?"

"I didn't have a choice, baby. *I. Didn't.*"

"What do you mean? Of *course* you had a choice."

"Well, if she were the mother you imagine, or the one you *deserve*, it would have been easy." She leans forward, and it sounds like she's begging. "I miss her, too, you know."

I stop pacing and look at Grammy.

"Mellie—your momma—had many special gifts. She was smart and caring and funny—but those parts of her got lost. And even if she isn't here now, you carry the good parts of her inside."

"I don't *want* to carry her inside. I want her to paint my toenails and show me how to put on makeup and just have a mom like everyone else does."

That hurts her, I can tell.

But I hurt, too. My heart and my body ache from the anger. I try to storm past her, but she follows me. "I was *trying* to stand *by* you. You needed *someone* to," she says.

"*That's* what you call standing *by* me?"

"Yes."

"Did she want me?" I ask, not sure which answer I want anymore.

"Yes. She did. She loved you, Delsie. But she wasn't able to be responsible for you. So, we all—Henry and Esme and me and Papa—decided to keep you safe here."

My fingernails digging into my palms begin to sting.

"I know this isn't easy to understand. But it was because we loved you. You're my *girl*. My Delsie."

Everything hurts from shoving away all this stuff that makes me sad inside. I want to blast her, but she already looks broken. I want to tell her I'm not *her* girl. I'm my *mother's* girl. And that it's her fault that I'll never be any-one's daughter. Ever. I want to hurt her, this Grammy I love so much.

But I can't.

I think of my mom and imagine her walking down our driveway and leaving Dennis Port. Knowing that someday I'd be old enough for her leaving to really hurt me. I know *she's* the one I'll really never forgive.

Chapter 22

OPTIMISTIC ELEPHANTS

After our argument, Grammy and I act like nothing happened, which is fine, I guess. I know sometimes Grammy has a hard time talking about things, but I can tell she's not mad at me, and I'm not mad at her.

Still, it feels good to get out of the house when Esme invites me to lunch. She looks beautiful when she comes to get me. She has her purple heels on and her Afro is in a sideswept updo, but there's one thing she doesn't have that surprises me.

"Where's Ruby?"

"Your grammy's going to watch her," she says, reaching for my hand. I take it, and I smile.

Esme and I slide into her car and head toward Route 6A, which Grammy calls Captain's Crunch because of the string of captains' houses and weekend traffic in the summer.

We pull into the parking lot of a yellow house called the Optimist Café. Esme turns the car off and then holds up one finger, telling to me to stay put. She runs to my side of the car and opens the door for me.

"Now, this is a fine tea house, and they have some darn good food, but there's something else I think you'll really like."

We are seated at a corner table, and Esme immediately takes her silverware out of the fancy cloth napkin and spreads the napkin on her lap. I do the same.

"So they have a bunch of fruit teas that you'll like. And the crepes are delicious."

"What's going on?" I ask. "Is something wrong?"

Her eyebrows scrunch. "No. Why would you think something is wrong?"

"I don't know . . . I just . . . I don't know . . ." My voice trails off like a bird flying away from the shore. "You don't usually ask me to get dressed up and take me out. I'm even wearing shoes."

"Well, it *must* be a special day." She smiles.

"Is there a reason you're taking me out? Do you have bad news or something?"

"Goodness no! We used to go out. When you were younger. And I guess I realized that we hadn't been out in a long time. And I've missed it."

"Oh."

"So," she begins. "How *are* things?"

I have a feeling she knows the answer.

She waits for me. And that's how it is with Esme. She'll ask a question she knows is hard to answer, and the air is filled with nothing but her waiting and smiling while you try to figure out what to say.

"Okay, I guess," I finally answer. Too much to explain.

And I like that Esme doesn't press me. She knows I'll talk when I'm ready. Being with her is a relief in a world where holding on to people feels like trying to hold on to wet fish.

I look around and do a double take at an odd painting— and then realize that the room is filled with them.

"Geez. Weird paintings," I say, staring at a goofy-looking boy and girl holding hands and coming down a hill. Next to it, there's an egg wearing a man's suit and hat sitting on a wall with a bunch of happy soldiers all around.

She points. "Can you figure it out? Keep in mind we're in the *Optimist* Café."

I know what an optimist is. Henry and Esme are always calling themselves optimists and telling Olive to not be such a pessimist. That life is too short.

She points at the goofy boy and girl. "Jack and Jill went up the hill to fetch a pail of water, but Jack did *not* fall down and break his crown." Then she points at another. "And there." A girl with a bonnet who is surrounded by sheep. "Little Bo-Peep did *not* lose her sheep."

Corny, but I like them. I point this time. "What about that one?" I ask about a bridge with a clock tower behind it.

"I guess London Bridge is *not* falling down." She points at a far wall. "Little Miss Muffet enjoying a snack with a spider."

I turn and smile. "Cool. Very optimistic."

After a few seconds, I notice Esme's necklace. "Oh! You're wearing your elephant necklace I used to play with when I was little. Didn't I name it something dumb?"

She laughs. "Trunkie. But you know, you were only about three years old. So you were advanced for your age."

"I don't think so." I put down my menu and stare at the elephant, trying to come up with something to say. The waitress saves me by coming to take our order. After she leaves, I ask, "Why do you like elephants so much? I mean, they're not really cuddly like bears."

"Well, I don't know that I would cuddle a bear. But, yes, I do love elephants because they are very intelligent and empathetic. And"—she falls against the back of her chair—"I've heard that, in the wild, they react to humans like humans react to puppies. Like, they think we're cute."

"Really? I guess we are. All tiny and everything."

"And they are uncommonly sensitive. They mourn their

dead just like we do. In fact, I read a story about Lawrence Anthony, a man they called 'the elephant whisperer.' He was so kind to elephants, saving many of their lives. He had elephants stay at his home."

"At his *home*?"

"Well, I don't think they took up guest rooms or anything." We laugh. "Anyway, this kind man passed away, and two days after his death, about twenty-five elephants traveled for twelve hours and showed up at his house and stayed for two days and two nights. They stayed as if they were mourning his death."

"Wait. How did they know he'd died?"

"That's the thing. No one knows how they knew. They just showed up."

I sit thinking about that.

Esme rests her elbows on the table. "You know, though. One of the things I love *most* about elephants is when several elephant families live together, they all become one. The parent elephants look out for and protect all the babies, not just the ones born to them. Those elephants are smart enough to know that blood doesn't always make a herd. Love is a more powerful thing than that."

She holds my gaze as I try to figure out if she is telling me that she loves me. It feels like she is.

The waitress delivers some fruit and biscuits and other delicious things.

Staring at the berries, I screw up the courage to tell Esme what's been on my mind. "I've been wondering," I say. "Can I ask you a question?"

"*Any*thing."

"If something happened to Grammy, would you—"

Her eyes widen. "*Delsie!* Of *course* we would take you! You wouldn't be alone for even a second."

"It doesn't seem like there would be room for me."

She leans forward and locks eyes with me. "Sugar pop. We *always* make room for the things that matter."

The front door slams, and the woman at the desk asks, "Can I *help* you?"

"No, thanks. Just looking for someone," he says.

Ronan? Is that Ronan?

He blows right by the lady, who clearly wanted more detail. "Hey," he says, sliding into a chair.

"Ronan, right?" Esme asks.

"What are you *doing* here?" I ask.

"Your grammy said you were here."

"Did she tell you to *come*?"

He shrugs. "No. I just *did*."

"Would you like something to eat?" Esme asks. "It's on me. That is, if you're hungry. *Are* you? *Hungry*, I mean?"

I'm wondering what's up with Ronan. I like him, but his timing is the pits.

"Well, a little," he says.

Esme asks the waitress to bring another setting. "Help yourself to some of the pastries. There's plenty."

He reaches for a biscuit and some butter and licks his fingers.

Esme hands him a napkin. He tucks it behind the collar of his T-shirt so it hangs down the front of him like a bib.

"So, tell me, Ronan," she asks, "how long have you lived here? Are you a Caper or a lowly wash-ashore like me?"

"Naw, I just got here a couple of months ago."

"With your parents?"

He glances over at me. "Nope. Just my dad."

"Where is your mom?"

I sit up straighter, realizing that I don't know the answer. Where *is* his mom?

He looks at Esme and seems sort of flustered.

"Why do you want to know?" he asks.

"Oh, I'm sorry. I was just curious. You don't have to tell me. I was just making conversation."

He reaches for another biscuit. "She died," he says. "So I came to live with my dad. I never stayed with him before, but he's okay. Although he doesn't talk much. We're like two great white sharks just circling each other. He left a job on a swordfish boat to have me come. He says he misses it." He turns to me and points at my plate. "You going to eat that?"

I shake my head, not even knowing what he's asking about. I can't believe it.

"Wait," I say. "Your mom *died*?"

"Yeah. It was a big thing. You know. Anyway . . . does this place have chocolate milk?"

Even Esme doesn't know what to say.

"I think they do, Ronan," she says, studying him and looking all worried.

"Can I get some?" He doesn't blink, holding her gaze like his life depends on it.

"Sure. You can get some." She leans forward on her elbows. "Ronan?"

He looks up quick.

"Are you okay? Have you spoken to anyone about this?"

"Naw." He reaches for some jam. "I don't like to talk about that stuff. But I do talk to Delsie all the time. Did she tell you about Darwin, the crab that I threw back into the water?"

I laugh because I don't know what else to do. Things not making sense seems to make sense these days.

Poor Ronan. And here I've been feeling sorry for *myself*.

Chapter 23

A SHOVELFUL OF SAND

"Delsie!" Mrs. Fiester calls.

I stop. "Hi, Mrs. Fiester. How are you?"

"I'm good, but I really haven't seen you around for a while. What have you been up to?"

"Lots of stuff. Helping Grammy. Training for a 5K. And, you know, the summer."

"Well, Brandy has missed having you around. You should go find her. She's down on the beach."

I wonder if Brandy has told her that or if she is just doing the mom thing. Sometimes adults have no idea what's *really* going on.

"Okay, thanks," I answer, and turn toward the beach. She didn't say if Tressa was there or not; I pray she isn't.

It's a perfect summer day, and the beach is crowded. Colored umbrellas and beach chairs cover the sand like confetti. Boogie boarders ride the waves. Sandcastles line the water's edge.

I spot Brandy. Alone. Relieved, I start down the wooden steps to the beach, but by the time I'm halfway down, I see Tressa walking out of the waves with a boogie board. She sees me, so I don't feel like I can just turn and go now. Especially if Brandy has missed me at all.

"Hey," I say as I reach them.

"Hey, Dels," Brandy says, and that makes me happy.

Tressa smirks. "What are you doing here? Cleaning *rooms?*"

There's a girl getting buried in the sand right next to us. Her friends are slowly covering her up, and I can hear her whining, "Why can't one of you do this instead?"

"What's the big deal?" one of the kids asks.

"Don't be such a baby," snaps another. "You said you wanted us to do it."

"Hel-looo?" Tressa asks, pulling me back. "What are you *doing* here?"

The voice of the girl being buried bugs me. And I think about the day I had lunch with Brandy and Tressa. Or, rather, I didn't because I thought they'd make fun of my sandwich. I remember pretending to know things and like things I didn't just because I wanted them to like me.

Tressa laughs.

The girl behind me cries.

I hear Grammy's voice telling me they can't break me.

I stare Tressa in the eye and straighten my back. I step forward. "I'm *here* because I *live* here. The Cape is my home. And, yeah, I was cleaning rooms because that's what my grammy does here and she needed my help. She works hard and is a great person. *You* are not." I turn to Brandy. "And you . . . you are just disappointing."

Brandy goes from watching me to looking at her feet.

I turn away and walk over to the girl being buried in the sand. She stops crying and gazes up at me. This stranger standing over her.

"Listen," I say. "You can either stay there while they throw shovelfuls of sand on you or just climb out. *Your* choice. Not theirs."

Then I head toward the stairs, not even looking back at Brandy or Tressa. And it feels really good to step away from the shovels of sand they've been throwing on me for weeks and finally climb out of the hole.

Chapter 24

STORM

The meteorologists on TV sound happy and excited this morning. Which means that we are in for some pretty fierce weather today.

The morning is humid but nice. People are on the beach. So I head off to find Grammy and help her clean some bathtubs. With her knees, she often has me help with those. I hear people talking about the storm and how disappointing it is to get bad weather on vacation. I completely disagree. Although I've never been on a vacation. Why would we leave the Cape to go somewhere else? Olive says she hasn't been over the bridge since God was a boy. I guess that was a long time ago.

I turn on the Weather Channel in the room we're cleaning. The meteorologists are still delivering bad news like a party invitation. Severe winds. Torrential rain. Coastal flooding. Lightning.

All sound great to me, too.

"Grammy! I'll be right back," I say, running out to the grassy area. The sky right above is still blue. But the clouds in the distance are getting darker and moving our way quickly.

I run to the top of the wooden stairs and look down at the beach. Tressa and Brandy are lying on towels. Seeing Brandy makes me sad, and I get the funny thought that friendship is like boogie boarding. You have to learn when to hold on and when to let go. I feel better now that I've let go.

I do a double take when I look back up at the sky and see something I've only seen on weather shows. An enormous anvil cloud is out over the Atlantic. The edges of the cloud are crisp and defined. This means we are in for a serious thunderstorm and maybe even some waterspouts—tornadoes that form over the ocean and sometimes come up on land, dropping things they've sucked out of the sea as they travel.

I look down at Brandy and Tressa again. They are wearing their matching sunglasses; I wonder if I should warn them that they won't need those for long, but I don't have to—all of a sudden it gets really dark out, and people start fleeing the beach.

Tressa races by me, but Brandy stops. "This is wicked weather, Delsie. You aren't going to sit on the beach and watch this, *right?*"

"No. I *would*, but I can't. Grammy won't let me."

"Good," she says, before running to catch up with Tressa.

I'm happy and have a little hope that Brandy does seem to care and maybe we'll be friends again, after all. But as I watch her with Tressa, I accept that a friend who changes as much as the weather is no friend at all.

I look back toward the ocean. Cool air is blowing in, and Ronan's dad is taking down the American flag.

A woman shields her face as she runs with a book and towel across the grass.

A volleyball is pushed up the sidewalk by the wind.

I run to the steps. The anvil cloud is closer. I can see the rain coming down out over the ocean—a curtain of water. It's beautiful.

The waves come ashore like black claws. Hammers pounding the sand. The surf rumbles like thunder.

A beach umbrella is lifted out of the sand and tumbles down the beach. It flips end to end right over where Tressa and Brandy had been.

And then the sky cracks in two. The rain doesn't come slowly. It comes all at once in sheets.

I run to find Grammy. When I get to the cottage where her supply wagon is parked, I step inside. "The weather is super cool. I mean, I guess *some* people would say really bad."

"It sounds fierce," she says, her eyebrows scrunched up like dust bunnies. "I peeked out the window, worried where you were." She is running around finishing up her last room of the day. "We have to get home," Grammy says quickly. "Olive will be a wreck."

"*Olive?*"

"Storms. Remember? Olive is terrified of severe storms like this. I just called Henry; he's not answering his phone. Esme and Ruby are off Cape today. So we'll have to go to Olive ourselves."

"But I want to stay on the beach and watch."

She whips her head around. "I'd sooner paddle out to that storm in a metal skiff with a flagpole strapped to my back than leave you here to watch such a thing."

I know there's no point in arguing as we scurry across the lawn. But then I hear people talking about a kid who had been in the water and had called for help. How no one in their right mind would go out in the water on a day like this.

"It was probably that caretaker's kid," one says. "What's his name? He's always into something."

I stop. I look to the ocean.

"I think it was the caretaker who went in after him," the woman says.

I run. I run across the grass with Grammy yelling my

name all the while. Thinking of the day I first saw Ronan standing on the edge of the water during a storm. Did he go *in* this time?

I have never seen the surf like this. It pounds the jetties with such force that the water sprays straight up into the air, creating giant walls of water that soar and then come crashing down on the rocks. A beach chair rolls along the sand as if it wants to fly like a plane. The waves roar.

I don't see anyone in the water. No one is there. What has happened? The water is more white than dark now. It reminds me of teeth.

Grammy comes up behind me and tugs at my sleeve. "C'mon, Delsie. We *have* to go. Olive is probably losing her mind."

I don't want to leave, but Grammy looks panicked, and I wonder what kind of danger Olive is in. I scan the water one more time. No Ronan. No Gusty.

She tugs again, and I run with her, and we jump into the car.

"But Ronan. I can't just *leave* Ronan."

"We're going to have to trust that he had the good sense to stay out of the water and that he's okay. Olive needs us."

I immediately turn the radio to AM and set it for no station at all. There is static with no station but pops as well. The pops are lightning hitting the ground nearby. And there are a lot of pops. Dangerous.

The lightning cracks overhead, and Grammy jumps. "I would rather not be in a car during a lightning storm," she says.

"A car is one of the safest places to be. Just avoid falling trees."

She gives me a look and says, "I'll avoid the trees. I just hope they'll avoid me."

The rain feels like a car wash. Water hitting us from all directions. The tree branches whip in the wind. The smaller trunks bend.

Soon, it's hailing and it sounds like we are being pummeled with pebbles.

We drive into our circle, and a small branch blocks our driveway. I look up at Olive's Tree and pray it holds on. It would flatten one of our small houses if it ever fell down.

We pull right up to Olive's house and run to it. Grammy swings open the unlocked door.

Olive is sitting under her kitchen table. Her knees to her chest. "Oh, Bridget. You're here. I called Henry, but he didn't answer and—"

The wind doesn't howl. It screams.

The wooden house creaks. The wind feels angry. Like the walls will come apart.

I wonder about the barometric pressure again. Is this a hurricane? "I'm going to go check my weather station."

Grammy whips her head around. "Oh *no*, you're *not*. You've got a weather station right there," she says, pointing at the window.

Grammy reaches for Olive. "Come, Olive . . . *please*."

I have already opened the cellar door.

Olive doesn't want to come out from under the table. She shakes her head.

"Now, hush, Olive. Come with us. The cellar will be safer."

We all jump when something crashes against the side of the house.

Finally, Olive gets up and the three of us file down the basement steps.

We sit under the stairs in the basement because it's the safest place. Staring upward, all praying for the same thing, I suppose. That somehow this house will stay planted on the ground. I don't need any hugging, but Olive needs some. Grammy wraps her up, and it surprises me to see. Olive taking a hug like that.

The wind screams. We stay quiet. I worry and pray and think about Ronan, hoping that boy stayed out of the water during a storm.

Chapter 25

THE REEL OF MISFORTUNE

The world smells different after a storm.

We have no power or phones the next morning, and that has Grammy worrying she'll miss the Game Show Network for days on end.

I am itchy to get out and find Ronan, but Grammy won't let me go. She's worried about power lines being down.

"But I have to go find Ronan and see if he's okay."

Grammy smiles big, and I am annoyed. Until she looks past me, waves her hand, and Ronan steps inside.

Before I think about it, I give him a quick hug. He doesn't know it's because I'm happy he is alive.

He straightens and looks at me like I just coughed up a quahog. "Hey, Delsie." His face is red.

"Sorry. I'm just . . . I'm just so happy you're okay."

"Why would I *not* be okay?"

"I heard you were in the water during that storm and your father had to go in after you. Is that true?"

"Heck no. But my father did go in after some other kid who drifted out on his inner tube and couldn't make it back in. I didn't see it, but it was pretty hairy, I guess. The kid's mother cried all over my dad, and now they're calling him *Gutsy* Gale instead of Gusty. Which he hates. I mean, *hates*."

I can see how Ronan feels about it. "That's cool. You must be proud, huh?"

"Yeah. Yeah, I am." He laughs. "But don't tell him I told you. You'd think he robbed a bank the way he wants to keep it a secret."

I laugh. "Okay. I won't."

"Man, but the storm was wild, huh? Freaky."

"Wild, yes. I loved it!"

"Most people would take a sunny day, you know. You're kind of alone on this."

"I've always loved wild weather. When I was little, I used to like watching the wind out the window pushing things around the yard. It seemed like magic for things to just swirl around by themselves. And my papa loved weather, too. We put up our own weather station, and we'd go out every morning to check it. He got me lots of weather books, too, so I could read about what makes the wind and stuff."

"Yeah," he says. "So, what causes wind, then?"

"Air moving in and out of different pressures. But all the while, the earth rotates underneath. So the wind gets pushed around. I used to wonder if the wind would get annoyed by that."

"Yeah, the wind gets mad. That's when you get a hurricane."

"Funny, Ronan, but *no*. You need really low barometric pressure for *that*."

He rolls his eyes. "Of *course* you do." Then he shakes his head. "But it's pretty cool how smart you are, Delsie."

"Thanks for noticing," I say.

"So," he says, "have you been down the other end of the beach? There's something kind of cool. You want to see it?"

I nod.

After Ronan assures Grammy that there are no power lines down near us, we jog toward Seagull Beach. As we run through puddles, water splashes all around us like it's raining up from the ground. Everything but the tops of our heads is soaked when we get there. There is a small crowd of people. And a boat.

"See?" Ronan says. "An abandoned boat. Since you're into that kind of thing."

"What do you mean?"

"Well, don't you take pictures all over the place of things left around? Towels and stuff?"

He's noticed that? I'm embarrassed. That is, until I recognize the boat. It's the only multicolored fishing boat that's ever pulled up to Chatham Pier.

"Oh no!" I yell. "That's Henry's boat!"

"*What?*" Ronan looks at the boat again. And he looks worried.

"Henry?" I yell. "What's happened to Henry?"

"Well, he can't be on the boat with it on its side like that, right?"

We both look toward the ocean. He wasn't answering his phone yesterday. And I haven't seen him today.

I start to run. Not toward the boat but toward Henry's house. And Ronan is right on my heels.

• • •

I jump up onto Henry's porch and bang on the door several times, wait, and bang some more. Finally, I yell, "Henry! Are you home? HEN-ry?"

No answer. I lean my forehead against the door.

"We should call the police," Ronan says. "Or the coast guard."

"They would have done that on the beach already. But I have a place we can check."

"Where?" Ronan asks, but I am already running.

"Saucepan Lynn's," I say. "It's his favorite place to eat breakfast."

With Ronan on my heels, I run through several back-yards and down Old Wharf Road to a tiny café behind the post office where the locals eat.

The creaky door slams as we walk in, and the regulars at the counter all turn to look at us.

"Henry!" I yell. "You're alive!"

He laughs. "Was I dead? The bacon hasn't gotten me yet."

"I couldn't find you and I know Esme and Ruby aren't home."

"Well, Ruby and her mom are away for a couple of days. And I didn't realize I'd been hiding anywhere." He smiles as he takes another bite of scrambled eggs.

I want to hug him, but I guess I need to stop hugging people and telling them I'm glad they're not dead.

"Sit down with me and have some breakfast."

"Henry!" I say. "We can't now. The *Reel of Fortune* has been beached!"

"*What?*"

"It's down on Seagull Beach."

He is wide-eyed and stops chewing to ask, "You sure?"

"*Henry,*" I say, "it was Papa Joseph's boat. I *know* what it looks like!"

Henry stands and fumbles with his wallet and throws

some money on the counter. "Let's go," he says, stepping over a dog and heading for the door.

• • •

Henry's truck slides on the sand as he pulls into the parking space and slams on the brakes. He's out and running before we are. When he sees the boat, he stands with both hands on top of his head.

"Captain Ahab!" he yells. "Here, Captain Ahab! C'mere, boy."

Ronan leans closer. "You didn't tell me he was nuts," he says.

I knock Ronan with my shoulder and point at Henry, who's scooping up a cat with three white legs and one black one.

Captain Ahab must be the only cat in the world who loves the water. He's one of the reasons I've spent hours trying to talk Grammy into getting me a kitten. On long fishing days, Captain Ahab is someone to talk to. Henry took him home once, but he yowled the entire night. Henry figures that cat doesn't know it should be terrified of the ocean and maybe just loves the smell of striped bass.

"Aye, matey." Henry sounds like a pirate as he talks to the Captain. "Have you run our boat aground in search of yer favorite fish?" Then he puts the cat down on the sand, and while the cat does figure eights around his ankles, Henry lets out a sound like a giant with a toothache. He rakes his own hair with his fingers and looks to the sky. "Well, boats aren't meant for beaches, so let's work on getting her back in the water."

Ronan steps forward. "We can wait until the tide comes in and push her back to sea."

"Well, Ronan, that's the right idea, but we'll need a bunch of help. If we try to move it ourselves and get an unexpected surge, someone could end up a permanent part of my boat," Henry says, chuckling. When times are toughest, he finds reasons to laugh. He takes out his phone and moves a few steps away while he talks.

"So," Ronan begins, "that was your grandpa's boat?"

"Yeah. The *Reel of Fortune*, for fishing and because Grammy loves game shows."

"Huh. That's funny. Why is it all different colors?"

"Papa Joseph painted it a different color every year, knowing that it would chip and reveal different colors underneath. He said it was a good reminder that everyone carries a lot of history with them. He thought chips and dents made a person more interesting."

I expect Ronan to give me some wise guy answer, but instead he looks me in the eye and says, "I wish I'd met your papa."

Henry returns. "So I've got some lads with boats coming. We'll get the *Reel* back on the water." Henry puts his hand on Ronan's shoulder. "But as Ronan points out, we'll have to wait until the tide comes in."

Ronan stands taller.

"Yep," Henry says. "We'll just wait for nature. She put us in this predicament and will help get us out. No use shouting at the rain. No one was hurt." He reaches over and rubs my back. "The *Reel* is tipped on the beach here, but I don't see any damage. And Captain Ahab is here to live another day of the eight lives he's got left."

Chapter 26

A BIT OF DRAMA

Ronan and I are talking about our strategies when it comes to Monopoly. We both believe in *buy everything you can*. But I leave the utilities behind because you can't build houses and hotels on them and I like to build houses and hotels. Lots of them.

"Delsie!" I hear a familiar voice I have missed. It's Aimee. And Michael is with her. They're coming up the driveway.

"Who are they, again?" Ronan asks.

"Aimee and Michael. My friends who are in the Cape Playhouse play this summer."

"Oh," he says, biting his nail.

I jump up and run to them, giving them both hugs. It feels good to have my old friends back. "What are you doing here?"

Aimee is staring at Ronan and then looking at me. I

know her well enough to understand that she is questioning why he is here. After that day of watching him at Sundae School.

"Are you the kid from Sundae School?" Michael asks.

"From Sundae School? I don't live there, if that's what you mean."

"No, of *course* not. You were there that day."

Ronan gets squinty-eyed in a nervous kind of way. "*What* day?"

I interrupt. "We were all there one day when you were, but we didn't really know you yet. We only knew that you and your dad had just moved here."

"Oh."

"So, what are you two doing?" Aimee asks.

"Playing Monopoly."

"The real version or your homemade one?"

"Why would I buy one if I have one?" I ask.

"Oh no! I get it," she says. "With not enough money and with houses and hotels that fall over. I think it's perfect!" And she gives me a shove and a look only a friend who's known you forever could give you. She knows my mom made that game and I'll never get rid of it.

"So," Aimee continues, "do you want to hit Cape Bowl? The playhouse gave us a ton of tokens for the machines and free bowling game coupons. I think it's so the kids who don't live here can check things out. But we got some, too."

"I mean, we don't have any money," I say.

Aimee shoves me a bit. "I know. I told you. We've got tons."

So, we all head up to Cape Bowl, where there is an arcade, a bowling alley, and a snack bar.

Michael swings open the door and lets us all walk in ahead of him.

We decide to bowl first. When we get up to the counter to get shoes, Ronan hangs back. "I don't need any shoes. I'll just wear mine."

"You can't," I tell him. "You have to get shoes."

He looks down at my feet. "Are *you* getting shoes?"

I reach into my pocket and pull out some ankle socks. "For bowling? Yeah. You have to have special shoes."

"Special shoes as in ugly shoes? Why can't I just wear mine?"

"You stumble if you wear yours. The bowling shoes slide."

Ronan looks a lot happier. "Slide? Cool."

We all get shoes, and Ronan stares down at his feet like he's grown an extra toe. But then he takes a running start and slides down the lane about six feet.

I go first, and Ronan watches everything I do. I get seven pins, but Aimee claps like I hit eleven.

While Michael is walking over to pick up a ball, Aimee starts to yell, "Brandy! Over here!" Then she turns to me. "*Look*, Dels. Brandy is here."

I turn slowly, not happy about who I'm going to see. I haven't had a chance to tell Aimee about the situation with Brandy and Tressa. And now they're heading our way. Turns out they are assigned to the lane next to us. How did I get so unlucky?

"Hey," I say.

Brandy seems unhappy to be next to us but says hi back. They begin to put on their shoes.

"Okay," Ronan says. "How hard could it be? You just stick your fingers in the three holes and throw the ball at the pins."

"Well, you roll it. Not throw it," I say.

Tressa laughs, and I'm thankful I don't have to see her much.

Ronan takes a running start and swings the ball out in front of him, but doesn't let go. He flies into the air and lands in the lane with a loud thud. Everyone turns. Brandy and Tressa laugh. Michael and Aimee laugh, too, actually. I mean, when I see he isn't really hurt, it's hard not to laugh. I've never seen anyone launch themselves down a lane before.

"Are you *okay*, Ronan?"

"Yeah, you think you're a human bowling ball, or what?" Tressa asks.

"Be quiet," I say. I wonder if Ronan is going to get mad. Michael stands and reaches out a hand to help Ronan.

Aimee comes over and whispers, "What is going on with Brandy?"

"She went to the dark side. Following that other one."

"That's too bad."

"Tell me about it."

I turn to Ronan. "Do you want to go play video games?"

"No. Why would I want to do that? I'm just getting the hang of it."

"Oh . . . yeah. I actually thought you might be . . . um . . . embarrassed?"

"You didn't like my first turn? What was wrong with it?" He raises his eyebrows. Trying to look innocent.

"It was great. A few more feet, and you could have hit the pins . . . with your *head*."

The four of us laugh.

It takes Ronan four turns to hit two pins, and he jumps around like he got a perfect game. Pumping his fists. Spinning around.

"This kid is a goof," Michael says. "He kind of grows on you, though."

"Like mold that grows on old food," Tressa chimes in.

I glare. "Who asked you?"

"Oh, did we hurt his feelings?" Tressa asks.

I turn to Brandy, who acts like she's not paying any attention to us. "Do you even speak anymore? Or are you not allowed?"

"Be quiet, Delsie."

"Clever comeback," I say.

Ronan steps forward and stands closer to Tressa and Brandy. "I've learned a lot this summer. One thing is that when you're hurt, it means you care. So, here is a question for you. If I'm not hurt, what does that mean?"

"C'mon," Tressa says to Brandy. "Let's go get snacks."

I know that watching Brandy walk away will stick with me for a long time.

I'll miss the friend she was—and could have been. But as Ronan makes Michael and Aimee laugh behind me, I think about how loyal these three are. I guess some friends are just glitter, and some friends are glue.

Chapter 27

WHATEVER FLOATS YOUR BOAT

There is a knock on the door. I can tell it's Henry just by how much the screen door rattles.

"Hey, Delsie! How are you?"

"Good. I'll get Grammy."

"No. Actually, I'm here to talk with you."

"You are?"

"Yeah," he says, folding his arms. "What's the weather look like tomorrow?"

"Eighty-two degrees. Moderate humidity. Decent barometric pressure, which is good. Winds out of the east at only about six miles per hour. Quiet day," I say. "But I know you knew that, so what gives?"

"Well, I didn't know quite *that* much." He laughs. "I just wanted to hear you say it. I knew you'd have the report." He unfolds his arms and stuffs his hands in his pockets.

"So it sounds like a pretty perfect fishing day. No wind. No weather. No surprises, which I know you'll like."

I'm so excited. I know what he's going to ask.

"So, I'm wondering if you'd like to come out with me. You're older now, and I think it's about time. Are you up for it?"

I jump once. "I would *love* it!" I clasp my hands together as if to pray. "But I told Ronan I'd hang out with him. Can he come with us? Please, please, please?"

"Fine with me. Provided his dad says it's okay."

I hug Henry, and he laughs again. Then he leans through the doorway and yells, "Bridget! Did you hear that? Can I take your girl fishing tomorrow?"

Grammy appears in the doorway. "How's the weather, Henry?"

"It's going to be as quiet as a seal on Monomoy Island."

"Okay, Henry. But you take care of my girl, you hear?"

"You know I'll take care of her just like she's mine."

I smile at Henry and leave for Seaside Heaven.

• • •

Ronan's drinking orange soda when he opens his door. "Hey," he says between gulps.

"Henry Lasko says he'll take us both fishing tomorrow if your dad says it's okay."

Before he can say anything, his father calls, "Ronan! Who's at the door?"

"It's just Delsie."

"Just Delsie? That's no way to greet someone, Ronan." His father steps up to me. His hair is a mess, and his face is scruffy, covered in whiskers. He smells like bacon.

He waves me in.

The house is dark, and there are clothes all over the backs of the chairs. There are some wooden fish hanging on the wall and a poster of a Portugal map over the couch.

Ronan seems uneasy.

"So what brings you by, Delsie?" his dad asks.

"Henry, my neighbor, wants to take me and Ronan out on his boat fishing tomorrow, but he said you have to give permission."

"Who is this Henry guy? How big is the boat? Does he have experience on the water?"

"He's a striper fisherman out of Chatham, and he's kind of like my dad," I tell him. "I don't know exactly how big his boat is, but it could probably hold, like, five couches."

He laughs. "A practical girl. I like that." He turns to Ronan. "Is this the boat you found beached that day?"

Ronan nods.

"Well," he says, "leave me this Henry's number, and I'll give him a call."

"Really?" Ronan asks. "You have to *call*?"

"Hey. I don't know the guy. I want to feel him out. I

wouldn't loan my car to a stranger. You think I'd send off my son? Out on the ocean, no less?"

• • •

"I'm glad he pretty much said yes," Ronan tells me, but now all of a sudden he's looking worried.

"What's wrong?" I ask.

"I don't have stuff to go fishing. I don't have a pole, and I don't have clothes for it. You know I don't even have a bathing suit."

"I don't think it matters. If you wear jeans and long sleeves on the boat, you'll look just like Henry and most of the other fishermen—and me. I burst into flames if I'm out in the sun all day. It's called an Irish tan. We bring fire extinguishers to the beach."

He rolls his eyes. "*Okay*, I get the point."

I shove him a bit. "And Henry has stuff for us to fish with. C'mon. It will be fun. If you don't say yes, I'll have to invite Tressa and Brandy."

"Okay, okay. I can't let you bring a couple of sharks to a fishing party!"

Chapter 28

SHARK SNACK

When Henry and I pull in to pick up Ronan, it's still dark outside. "Well, hello there, Ronan! Glad to have you aboard! Sorry about the time. Got to go when the tides are just right."

"Thanks for inviting me."

For a long time, we drive in silence on empty, dark roads, until Henry finally says, "So, Ronan, you said your dad had a lot of experience on the water. Perhaps you'll take to it, too."

"He did. He was a swordfish fisherman before I came. He'd be out for weeks at a time."

Henry heads up the hill toward Chatham Pier. "That's a tough life. Takes a lot of guts."

"Yeah," Ronan sighs. "He misses it. He says that a lot. I think he wants to go back to it."

Henry stares at Ronan as he pulls the key out of the ignition. I think he's going to say something, but instead, he pushes open his truck door and we all get out. Then he reaches into the back and pulls out two life vests. "Put these on."

"I don't need that," I say. "I don't like those things."

"Well, you don't have to wear it, then. You'll be more comfortable, I'm sure."

That was easy, I think.

"I mean," he continues, "you'll be sitting on the dock waving to Ronan and me as we head out to sea. But you'll be more comfortable."

I take the vest and put it on while Ronan laughs.

When Henry starts the *Reel*, I feel a jolt and rumbling through my feet. I look at the captain's wheel and half expect to see Papa Joseph wearing his hat with the flaps on the side and back to shield him from the sun. His T-shirt had a salty fisherman on the back that said CALL ME JOSEPH.

It isn't long before we head around Monomoy. Ronan points. "Hey! Look at all the seals!"

"Yeah," Henry says. "Monomoy is one of the best restaurants on the Cape for great whites. No reservations required."

"Cool." Ronan lights up. "Maybe we'll see great whites. I love great whites."

"That's because you're not a seal," I say, watching the

seals lie on the sand. I wonder if the madre and her baby are there somewhere.

When we hit the open ocean, Henry turns on his GPS and fish finder. I'm surprised at how detailed they are. Like watching a TV screen.

Ronan leans in and studies it. "Look, Delsie! Look at the fish there."

"Not quite the ones we're looking for," Henry sighs. "Probably a big school of mackerel. If I were looking for bait today, that would be great, but we want to nab bigger stuff."

"How can you tell what kind of fish it is?"

"Ah . . . the size. The depth. And the depth in terms of the sun, too. As the sun gets higher in the sky, the stripers go deeper. That's why we're out here so early."

In the distance, a bunch of seagulls are dive-bombing the surface of the water—a sure sign that there are fish there. As we get closer, we see there are rips.

When we get to the spot, the birds are angry but Henry is happy. "We're right over a shoal. And I think we're looking at some stripers here on the screen. Let's get fishing and see if we can get them in the boat."

Henry flips open a plastic box. Inside there are live eels. I remember they are his favorite bait for catching stripers.

Ronan reaches in and picks one up.

"Good. Not squeamish. Good way to begin."

I plunge my hand into the box and grab an eel, too. A bigger one than Ronan's.

"It's going to be a lucky day. I can feel it," Henry says. "So you two want to bait your own hooks?"

I hesitate, since the eel is looking at me, but I think of my momma, and I want to be at least as good as her at this. Even better.

"Yes, I can do it. Just show me how."

Henry grabs an eel and puts the hook through one eye and out the other so it holds. He then holds up the eel, which makes the letter J, telling him it's still alive. "Yup. Good solid hold there," he says. "A striper will attack its prey from the front, so the hook will have a good chance of catching the striper that way."

Ronan baits his hook. So do I, and it's gross. But I don't let on.

"Good things come to those who bait," Henry says.

"Unless you're an eel," I say. "So now I cast?"

"Naw. No casting for stripers. You just drop it in the water off the side and then jig it. Move it up and down."

"Here, fishy, fishy," I say.

Henry shakes his head.

"Okay," he says. "If you feel like you've got a nibble, count to three. Slowly. And then yank the line. If you yank too soon, you'll probably pull the hook out of the fish's mouth. You've got to be patient."

And it turns out that being patient is important, as we sit for over an hour with no nibble from anything. We can't make a lot of noise, either, because Henry says that scares off the fish.

But finally. *Finally*, I get a nibble, and I count to three. One Mississippi, two Mississippi, three Mississippi. And yank.

"Great, Delsie! You set the hook!" I think Henry is happier than I am.

But the fish isn't. It yanks back. Hard. And we see it come out of the water, curling, as it fights back.

"Let me help you, Delsie," Henry says.

"*No.* I'm going to do it myself."

"Oh boy." He laughs. "I heard your mom say that to your papa many times."

I'm both happy and sad to hear this.

With Henry's directions, I pull the pole back behind my head and then crank the reel, moving the pole forward, never letting the line get slack. Move back, crank the reel, move pole in front of me. Pull back and repeat.

By the time Henry plunges the net into the water to scoop up the fish, my arms are so tired, I can hardly lift them. But I did it myself. I caught my own fish. And I wish Grammy and Esme had been here to see it.

We measure it, and Henry says, "Whoa! A forty-incher! You don't start off small, that's for sure. I'm guessing about twenty-three pounds. At about three dollars a pound, you've just earned about seventy dollars."

"Wait. What?! I get to keep the money?"

"You'll get to keep whatever we sell it at. That's a good estimate."

I jump up. "Yes!"

Henry hoists the fish into the huge cooler filled with ice.

Ronan is happy for me, I can tell. But I can also tell he really wants his own fish. Henry puts his hand on Ronan's shoulder. "Okay, son. Let's pull out the big guns. My lucky St. Croix. One of the best fishing poles around."

I turn around. "St. Croix? Isn't that where Esme was born?"

"Indeed. Unique, beautiful island. Smart, beautiful lady."

Henry offers to help Ronan, but he wants to do it himself.

With the first nibble, Ronan yanks too quickly and loses the fish.

"Happens to the best of us," Henry says.

Later, I catch another striper that's only thirty inches long, and Henry says we have to throw it back. It's too small to keep.

Ronan gets another bite and he counts to three and then yanks his pole to the side, setting the hook in the fish's mouth.

When the fish breaks the surface, we see it's an enormous

one, and Ronan breaks into the biggest smile I've ever seen on him.

"Now, when you get this one in the boat, this sucker will be a great picture for your dad."

Ronan looks sad but brightens to agree. I can tell he's faking.

Henry stands behind him with a slight smile and the ocean reflecting off of his glasses, and I feel thankful for him. Thankful that he took us out and thankful just to know him.

Ronan is cranking the reel on the St. Croix. Pulling back. Cranking again. Pulling back.

"Well, Delsie, I think this may be as big as yours! But it's hard to hold on to the pole. Man, this thing is heavy."

"Seventy dollars' worth of heavy," I say, smiling. "We'll go to Saucepan Lynn's and have all the pancakes we can eat!"

As Ronan laughs, his pole is yanked hard—a great white shark comes out of the water like a rocket off a launchpad. It comes up from underneath the fish with its mouth wide open, soars upward, nabs the fish, and then falls back into the ocean, almost on its side. It all happens so fast that it takes me a few seconds to realize Ronan has let go of Henry's prized St. Croix fishing pole. It's about ten feet from the boat and moving away from us.

Ronan takes two running steps toward the side of the

boat, ready to jump over, I think. But Henry is able to grab ahold of his life jacket and pull him back.

Henry is wide-eyed, looking at him. "What are you *doing*, Ronan? It's just a fishing pole."

"I can cut the line," he says.

"Just because you *can* do something doesn't mean you *should*."

"I'll help the shark. Get the St. Croix back for you. He won't be interested in me. Great whites don't attack people. Very rarely. I'm more likely to get killed by a vending machine. Or a cow. More cows attack people than sharks, and no one freaks out about them."

"*What?*" Henry is confused. "It's a *shark*. A great *white*."

"Seriously. Statistically, it's more likely I'd get killed by a vending machine or a cow than a shark."

"Listen, kid. You really—"

"Please?" Ronan interrupts. I've never heard him sound like that before. Like a little kid begging.

"You can't do that, son. You saw that shark who took your fish. He's still around somewhere."

"I could be fast. I'll cut the line and grab it quick!"

Looking out at the water, I notice the pole is gone now. "I think it's too late anyway, Ronan." Ronan's face is hard like a rock. "I'm sorry you lost the fish. I'll split my money with you."

"But your pole. The St. Croix is your lucky one. I'm so sorry. I want to get it back for you," he begs Henry.

"It's just a pole," Henry says, stepping forward. "It's okay."

And Ronan steps back. "I didn't mean to let it go. If I—"

"It's really okay, Ronan. Relax. It wasn't all that lucky, anyway."

Henry reaches out to touch his shoulder, but Ronan leans just enough away to avoid it.

"Things happen," Henry says. "Better the pole go in the water than one of you."

"I'm so sorry," Ronan repeats. He sits down on the deck with his back against the side. His knees are up near his chest, and his forehead rests against his palms. Then he looks up to say one more thing to Henry. "Please don't tell my father. What kind of fisherman would want me for his kid?"

Chapter 29

THE GREATEST PREDICTOR OF SUCCESS

The next morning, Ronan and I head to Saucepan Lynn's for some pancakes. Saucepan Lynn is also a volunteer fire-fighter, so she cooks in her suspenders in case she has to run off.

I remember the day she slapped a handful of keys on the counter and told the regulars to take one. That they could start pulling their weight around the place and get in early to help with breakfast. One of Henry's favorite things to do is leave the house before dawn and get some bacon frying on the griddle.

When we arrive, we have to step over a couple of golden retrievers. When some people complained about them, Saucepan hung up a sign that says IF YOU HAVE A PROBLEM

WITH OUR DOGS, WE ARE HAPPY TO RECOMMEND ANOTHER
RESTAURANT.

We sit at the counter, and Ronan is mesmerized watching Saucepan. "Man, she's got some arm muscles on her." He leans over and whispers, "What's her tattoo of?"

"A ship's anchor with a saucepan hanging off the bottom. When she flexes her muscles, the pan swings back and forth a bit."

"That's wicked cool." He laughs.

"And on her wrist she has the Yarmouth firefighter badge. Most firefighters in town have one."

Saucepan reaches over and gives a rubber chicken a few squeaks. That's the signal for the waitresses that there are meals to deliver. Then she resumes an old argument with the regulars. "There are worse things than spending a day on a boat. I hang over a hot stove."

"Oh, c'mon! Are you *kidding* me?" one of the guys shoots back. "In January, the wind makes your bones crack. I'd give my teeth to stand over a hot stove. *And* no one has ever died making sauce."

"Well," she says, "you can yammer on about bones cracking, but if there's a few sprinkles out, I see you *here* hunched over a hot cup of coffee. And I hear you bragging about the patience you have in catching fish. You want to know about patience? Try making a fine sauce."

"What's sauce got to do with patience?" another regular asks.

"*Everything!*" she bellows, pointing her whisk at him. "A good cook knows you can't go turning up the heat because you're impatient; you gotta let it simmer. Take its time. Let all of those flavors come into their own. Because if you rush it . . . well, it won't satisfy. *But . . .*" She leans forward. "If you cook it just right, folks can't shake the memory of it and long for another taste. *That's* what brings them back."

"You *mean* to tell *me*," a fisherman says, "that you think that it takes more patience to cook a sauce than to fish on the ocean when you can't see land in any direction and you're out there for hours in all kinds of weather? Dealing with seasickness and engine troubles and any number of other things that happen?"

"Yeah. Because a sauce takes time and love. Once you catch the fish, the job is done. God's done all the work for you."

Amid the grumbling of a bunch of fishermen, she whips her head around to look at us. "*Hey!*" she says, pointing at Ronan. "Is your name Ronan?"

"Uh . . . *yeah?*" he says, pushing his chin forward.

"You ever flipped a crepe?"

"A crepe?"

"Yeah, a crepe. It's like a very thin pancake, and we put fruit and other things inside."

"Why?"

"Just answer. You flipped a crepe before or not?"

Ronan turns around, I guess to check if there's someone behind him that she's really talking to.

When he turns back, she points at him again. "Yeah, I'm talking to *you*, short stack."

He spreads his feet apart. "*Don't* call me that."

She squints one eye. "Okay. I'm sorry. But don't you be worrying about how big you are. I've known plenty of big men who didn't have a drop of bravery. Being strong in the ways that matter has nothing to do with muscles. It's about the size of a man's heart and soul. Not his shirt size."

I think about Grammy's talking about Papa's strong shoulders and realize that I misunderstood what she meant.

She walks around the counter but holds Ronan's gaze. "So Henry Lasko was here this very morning talking about how brave you are, wanting to jump into the water after sharks—and by the way, I hope someone has told you that ain't brave. That's just foolishness. But this is what I want to know: Are you brave enough . . . to flip a good crepe?"

It startles me that the words *brave* and *crepe* are in the same sentence. I look at Ronan and think how he won't be able to resist her challenge. I'm betting that telling Ronan to stay away from a dare is like telling a seagull to stay away from a french fry.

He walks around the counter and over to the grill. "What am I supposed to do?"

She puts an oven mitt on his hand. "I've got two crepes ready to be flipped. I'll do the first. You do the second."

One of the fishermen yells, "What are you *doing*? Leave the kid alone!"

She snaps back, "Now, you just mind your own p's and q's there!" She turns to Ronan. "You want me to leave you alone?"

Ronan clears his throat. "*No.*"

Saucepan continues. "Good. Now, I think the way a person flips a crepe says something about who he is and his future."

He looks at her like a bass just swam out of her mouth.

"Yeah," she says, leaning in. "People look at me like that a lot. And I don't much care, to be honest. But I'm right about the crepes. Trust me."

She grabs the handle of the first pan and steps back from the stove. "Gotta put some muscle into it. Take control. Show the crepe who's boss."

"Wish I had a nickel for every time I've heard that," Ronan says.

"Hey. None of your funny business here."

He smirks.

She shakes the pan to loosen the crepe, then angles it downward and swoops it in a circle. The crepe flies into the air, flips, and lands in the pan. "Easy," she says, with a single nod. "Your turn."

Ronan gets squinty-eyed, and I worry for him.

"C'mon. Putting it off will only burn the thing."

"I'm not putting it off. I'm preparing."

"Well, prepare faster."

I hold my breath. Ronan seems so calm, but he grunts as he sends the crepe into the air.

The roar from the fishermen's laughter shakes the place.

Saucepan Lynn looks up at the ceiling. "You really stuck it up there, kid. You are strong, that's for sure." She leans toward the back room and yells, "Someone get me the broom!" Then she turns back to Ronan. "Well, perhaps you need a bit of finesse, but I think you'll do great things, kid."

Chapter 30

WAS MY MOMMA STRONG?

When I walk into the kitchen, Grammy's cleaning and our stove has been pulled away from the wall. Grammy is trying to shove it back into place. "I'm an ox, I tell you."

I laugh. "I don't know if you ought to go around telling people that. No offense."

"I'm just saying that I'm strong. Nothing wrong with that. You're strong, too, Delsie. All us McHill girls are."

"I don't know if I'm all that strong," I mumble.

She whips around. "Now, *none* of that talk. What do I tell you?"

I stand straighter. "That I better straighten my crown and remember who my grammy is."

"That's right, baby. Don't you worry. It's in our blood. We're like Esme's jars—with our strong shoulders."

I know Grammy likes her metaphors, and I think back

to her saying "Joseph is my rock." I'd always thought it was a weird thing to say about a person. I didn't really know what it meant until now. Papa's strong shoulders weren't just about him being able to pull wet ropes into his boat. It had to do with him being rock-solid for the rest of us. Always there. Keeping his promises. Protecting us.

And I can't help but wonder if my momma was weak.

I just have to ask.

"Grammy?"

"Yes, baby?" Her voice sounds like she's singing.

"Was my momma weak?"

Grammy stares out the window for a while before turning around. Her eyes are shiny, and I feel bad that I asked her. But, truly, I just have to know.

"Your momma was plenty strong."

"I mean . . . I don't mean weak arms. I mean like when you talk about Papa being strong. Loving us. Protecting us. I don't know. I guess . . ." I swallow hard. "I know she wasn't here long, but while she was . . . did she . . . you know . . ." I want to say *love*, but I'm afraid. "Protect me at all?"

"Your mother loved you," she says. Of course. Grammy always knows what I don't say.

"But, Grammy, you've always said that strong people can will themselves to do anything. Why did she leave me, then?"

"Strength comes in all kinds of forms, you know. I think your momma's strength came in leaving—not in staying."

I don't understand.

"Your momma . . ." She speaks slowly, as if the words make her hurt. "She lived in the bottle, but the day"—she points at the end of my nose and leans toward me—"the very *day* she found out you were coming, she stopped. She sweated with the fits and heaves. She curled herself up on the floor and moaned and called for God and the devil, but she swore that while you were growing, she'd die before taking a drop. That was the strongest I've ever seen anyone be."

I take a step back.

And Grammy takes a step forward.

"The day you came into this world, she looked at me with a sparkle in her eyes that I hadn't seen in too long of a time. 'Who could look at this baby girl and not believe in angels?' she asked me."

I look out our window at the abandoned house across from ours. "But she . . ." Then I turn to Grammy. "Then how come she didn't want me?"

"No, Delsie, no. That's not it. Oh, how she loved you. She just . . . she was sick. And you can't blame anyone for being sick."

I swing my head toward Grammy. Confused.

"When you came into the world, she never put you down for a solid week. When she starting drinking and drugging again, it ripped me up. She said you deserved better. She cried like she was dying. Like she didn't want to go but someone was making her. I don't know what was banging around that head of hers, but I *do* know that she left because she loved you—*not* because she didn't want to be your mother."

"Don't you wonder where she's gone to?" I ask.

"With every breath, baby. With every breath."

Chapter 31

EELS FOR THE REEL

The next morning, I'm surprised to see Ronan walking through our neighborhood. But he isn't coming to see me. He is heading to Henry's house. And he's carrying a plastic box.

I spring out the door. "Ronan!"

"Hey," he says. "You know if Henry's around?"

I shrug and then turn my head toward his house. "Henry!" I yell.

"Geez," he says. "I could have just knocked."

"What's in the box?" I ask.

"Something for Henry," he answers.

Henry steps onto the porch like it's the deck of the *Reel of Fortune* on a still-as-glass day. Hooking his thumbs in his suspenders. Taking a breath and looking up at the sky. "I love these stormy, windy days. Home with my girls and now a surprise visit from the two of you." He swings open the door. "C'mon in. I think Esme has some tuna sandwiches with your names on them."

Ruby stomps. "Hey! I want my name on a sandwich, too!"

Henry laughs. "My spitfire. Your name is on everything." And he winks, making her giggle.

We step inside and it's warm. Nice, since this day feels more like October than early August.

"Take a load off," Henry says to us as he motions toward the couch. Ruby plops herself on the floor and then spreads out on her back like a starfish. "So what brings you by?"

"I brought you something," Ronan says, holding the box out to Henry. "But you probably shouldn't open it inside."

Ruby sits up fast. "Will it bite?" she asks.

Ronan laughs. "Yeah. Probably."

"Coooool," she says, drawing out the word.

We step outside, and Henry opens the plastic box. It's filled with the fattest eels I have ever seen. I crack up laughing. Eels always have this expression like they just told a joke and they're waiting for the others to laugh.

"Hey!" Henry practically yells. "Nice! Where did you buy these?"

"I didn't buy them. I was up early and went out and caught them for you because I know you like eels to catch stripers, and I feel awful about losing your pole. I really do.

There's no way I can raise that kind of money anytime soon. But I thought these might help you pull in some extra fish."

"Thanks, Ronan," Henry says, putting his hand on Ronan's shoulder. "That was thoughtful of you."

"I'll pay you back someday. I will. I promise."

"It's okay, Ronan. This will cover it for sure. Just one more thing I need from you."

Ronan stands tall. "Anything."

"I don't want to hear about this pole again. I know you feel bad, but it was a mistake. We all make them, and the best we can do is try to make it right. And you have. So enough of this, okay?"

Ronan nods.

Chapter 32

OUTSIDE LOOKING IN

Grammy is going to be late from work, so I sit with my back against Olive's Tree, watching the Laskos' windows like they are television sets. I watch as Henry and Esme put things on the table to eat. I watch Esme draw her fingertips across Ruby's back as she rushes about. I see Henry laugh, and I am grateful that I can't hear it. And yet I long to . . .

I hear someone behind me step over the knee-high fence, but I can't take my eyes from the light that wants to both pull me in and lock me out at the same time. I thought Ronan had gone home.

"What are you doing back?" I ask. "Isn't your dad going to be mad?"

"I somehow doubt it," Olive says, with a bit of a *humpf* tacked onto the end.

When I turn, she is standing with her hands on her hips,

looking up at the top of the tree. "He's been long dead, so I don't imagine he'd be mad at anything. He would be mighty proud, though, of this tree that's been doing all this growing. When I was a girl, he used to cover it in Christmas lights a week before Halloween." She looks at me. "So what are you doing, anyway?"

"Nothing."

"Like your grammy says, when a person says 'nothing,' it's always something." Then she turns to see what I see and makes another sound. Not like her usual *humpf*, but different. Like a mini *aha*, which is surprising. Olive doesn't ever seem surprised about anything.

"He worked for General Electric."

I look up, wondering what I missed.

"My father. My father worked for General Electric, and did he ever love this tree. It was—and still is—the center of our little neighborhood. His company gave him new lights every year because he promised he'd gather up the store owners and invite them over to see how bright the lights really were. And he did.

"Halloween picnics. November cookouts. By December, he'd be out here in a parka grilling burgers, with Christmas carols blasting from the house. My mother said she thought he was crazy. But . . . she didn't really . . ." She lets out a long, slow breath. "We all loved it." Her head drops a bit. "I do miss them. They were good people. Not huggers or the types to go to pieces over loving someone. But good people."

She turns to me. "You know, some people love plenty but just can't show it," she continues. "Not like . . ." She looks over at the Laskos' house. "Esme—that woman has love bubbling over. She wears her affection for people like other people wear jewelry."

She's noticed that, too.

"Your grammy, though. She's busy. And she's getting on in years. You'd have to count all the waves in the ocean to know how much Bridget loves you. You're a lucky girl."

I stare up at her. She seems sad watching the Lasko show in the windows. "I envy them. I never learned how to do what Esme does."

And then I realize that she's out here looking up at the tree and missing her family, too. I have to catch my breath when I also realize that we're both orphans.

"What are your eyebrows all scrunched up for?" she asks. "Something spinning in that head of yours? You know it's a McHill tradition. Thinking about every little thing."

"I was thinking that we're both orphans, you and me."

She nods slowly. "Yes. Yes, we are." She sits down next to me. "Well," she says, "I suppose there is no arguing with facts."

"You knew my mother, huh?"

"What a silly thing to ask. You know I did. I was here

when Mellie came home from the hospital with Joseph and Bridget. God, how they loved that baby. Don't know why she . . ."

"She what?"

Olive looks disgusted again. "Well, what do you *think*?"

I should be upset, I guess, but I'm actually finding Olive to be a relief. I never have to wonder what she's thinking. I lock eyes with her. "Why she left?" I say.

"Of *course*. She was careless about things. Didn't think ahead. Didn't take responsibility. And I think that's caused some hard things for all of you. I'm sorry."

"Thanks, Olive."

"But you know what *else*?"

"Yeah?"

"I have faith in you. I bet one day you'll wear an olive wreath on your head, and people will cheer for you."

"Huh?"

"You know who gets the olive wreath up in Boston? The winner of the Boston Marathon."

I smile. I'm happy that she thinks I can do something special.

I hear Grammy's tires rolling up the driveway, so I stand and brush the pine needles off of my legs.

"You're a mess. Your grammy is going to make you bathe."

I sigh. "Yeah."

You can always count on Olive to point out the terrible stuff.

But I see her looking up at her tree the way most of us look at people we love, and I get the feeling that she isn't thinking about the tree. She's thinking about her father and their cookouts and the people she misses.

I think that when I look at Olive from now on, I'll see a lot of different things. Like instead of just a plain scoop of cold ice cream, a scoop with some chocolate chips hidden inside.

Chapter 33

THE HARDEST SHELL OF ALL

"You know how to go clamming?" Ronan asks before the front door is even open all the way.

"Yeah, why?"

"I wanna go. Do you have the cage things on a pole that they use?"

"You mean a clam rake? Yeah, we have some out back, I think. And baskets and a gauge. But . . . I have a permit. You *need* a permit."

"My father got me one. As a surprise. So I guess he wants me to learn clamming. So I'm asking you."

I nod once, thinking about how serious he is. Even for him.

"Well?" he asks. "Are you busy?"

"I guess not."

"Okay. Let's go, then."

We head to the cove just as the tide is going out. Holding the rake, Ronan looks like that famous painting of the farmers standing with a pitchfork. All serious.

"So what do we do now?" he asks.

"Follow me," I tell him.

We wade out into the bay. The surface of the ocean separates the two worlds of hot air and cool water. The tide is moving, so the sand whirls around my feet.

I stop when the water is up to my knees and turn to Ronan. "Okay," I say, pointing to the wire basket with a floatable noodle around the rim so it sits in the water, tied to me so it won't drift away. "This is called the peck. When you catch clams, put them in the basket. Being in the water gives the clams a chance to spit out sand and gunk. They'll be nice and clean by the time they're ready to eat."

I hold up the clam rake. "So you just take this and pull it through the sand like a regular rake. You'll catch all kinds of stuff. Then just dig through to see what you have." I grab ahold of the metal ring tied to the top of the rake. "This ring will tell you if it's big enough to keep."

I draw the long teeth through the sand, pull up a bunch of things, and dig through what I've got. I find two clams. "Here," I say, "put this in the peck basket. It's a keeper." I pick up the second. "This looks too small." It passes through the ring. "Yeah, not legal." And I toss it out into the water.

"Why do we have to throw back the small ones?"

"They are young. Besides, they aren't worth keeping anyway."

A weird expression flashes across his face.

"What?"

"Nothing," he says, suddenly moving around, digging here and there.

I follow him to the shallow water and help him. "Look for little bubbles; that means there's a clam underneath. Try to feel for them with your feet, too. Bumps under the sand."

I stand in a quiet spot and close my eyes. I take a step to the right, stand still, and close my eyes again. And then I feel it. The tiny little bump on the bottom of my feet that most people don't pay any attention to. A hiding clam. I reach into the sand with my fingertips and pull it out. I can tell by the looks of it that it's legal.

I walk over and drop it in the peck basket.

But Ronan isn't having any luck. "I thought this was easy," he says.

"Looking is half the fun."

"I'd rather just bring home a bunch of clams."

"A bushel. You bring home a bushel," I say. "Not a bunch."

His mouth is swung to the side. "*Whatever*. Bushel, then."

"If you're that impatient, head over there," I say,

pointing to an area of rocks to the side. "Grab a big rock and bring it back over."

He drops his rake and runs.

"You can't just drop things in the water, you know! They kind of float away!" I call as he goes.

Soon he returns with a big rock. "So?"

"Throw it at the wet sand. Then look for the bubbles."

He throws the rock in the sand just in front of his feet. There are bubbles.

"Quick!" I say. "Dig 'em up before they go deeper."

Ronan sinks his rake into the sand and pulls wet mounds toward himself. Then he bends over and pulls out two clams. Ronan pulling two clams out of the sand is like a pirate discovering a chest full of gold coins.

He runs around with the rock, darting back and forth, hitting the sand with it. Now I don't even look for clams. Watching him is far more interesting. But he doesn't seem like himself. He's like a clamming machine, and as he catches them, he stuffs them into the pockets of his new black cargo shorts.

"Ronan. You can't keep the clams in your pockets. They need to be underwater so they can spit the gunk out and clean themselves."

"Relax. You don't have to tell me what to do every second."

Huh? "I'm just trying to help you. The clams are gross if they don't get a chance to spit."

"Why don't you mind your own business?"

I stare for a few moments. "What is *wrong* with you? Why are you so *mad?*"

"Just leave me alone," he snaps.

I head toward shore. "Fine. I will."

He's watching me as I scoop up my stuff and splash as I trudge away.

He comes up behind me. "I'm sorry."

I turn.

"Hey, Delsie. Please don't go."

I stand silent.

"I got. A letter. From *her*. I got a letter from . . . my *mother*."

"*Wait. What?* Ronan . . . how could your mom write a letter? That doesn't really sound . . . Well, I don't know . . ."

He sighs. "She didn't *die*. I just said that. Because it's easier than explaining."

I can't believe it. He has a mother, and he tells people she *died?*

Ronan's voice reminds me of floodwaters. "She's alive, Delsie. I've wanted to tell you. We live—well, *lived*—in Worcester. And then one day, out of the blue, she just *sent* me here."

"Sent you here?"

"Yeah. *Sent* me here. She said . . ." His voice shakes as he continues. "She said she didn't want me around any . . . *anymore.* That I'm too much trouble, and . . . I mean, I do get in trouble. I don't know why. It's just like sometimes my body and brain aren't on the same team. But I never thought she'd . . ." He stuffs his fists into his pockets and drops his chin.

"I'm sorry, Ronan. She really said that? That's awful."

"She said it's because I'm about to become a teenager. She doesn't want one around. Too much to worry about, and she says I need a father to keep me in line." He swallows hard. "She thinks I'm bad."

"Ronan. You're not *bad.*"

"Yes, I am. She sent me a letter." His voice cuts. "Don't you under*stand* me?" He grows louder. "I was so happy when I saw her handwriting on the envelope. I thought it was a letter to say I could come home, but she said . . ." He kicks at the water. "She said that she hoped I was doing okay but it was all for the *best.*" He kicks the water again and takes a swing at nothing. Then, crumbling, he falls to his knees. "For the *best*?" he asks, pressing his arms against his stomach and curling forward. "What's *for the best* even *mean*, anyway?"

Something in the water gets his attention. He sniffs and

stares for several seconds. Finally, he asks, "What is that? It looks like an alien helmet."

I lean over. "That's a horseshoe crab. Cool to actually see one. We find their shells on Seagull Beach all the time."

"Their shells?"

"Yeah. They shed their shells the way snakes shed their skin."

"Huh. It would be cool to just shed something and swim away," he says, crawling on all fours and then picking up the crab. He examines the horseshoe crab and then turns it over. Ronan watches wide-eyed as the horseshoe crab waves everything wildly. "This one is definitely strong," he says. Then it bends into an L-shape and points its tail at Ronan.

"They are one of the oldest animals on earth," I say, touching one of its legs. "They literally swam around with the dinosaurs four hundred fifty million years ago."

"I love this thing!" Ronan counts the twelve legs with claws. "And what's *this*?" he asks, wiggling his finger over a mound of what looks like dead grass in the middle of its many legs.

"That's its mouth."

"*Sick.*"

Ronan bends over and places it back in the water as if it could break. He watches it scurry away.

Just then, two boys swim over to it, and the shorter one catches the horseshoe crab and holds it up. "*Cool!*"

The taller one, laughing, says, "I wonder if you pull its leg off, will it grow back, like starfish?"

Ronan stands.

The taller boy reaches over and grabs ahold of one of the crab's legs.

I had no idea Ronan could move that fast. Before I know it, he hits one kid and pushes the other. The horseshoe crab splashes into the water and swims away.

One of the kids pushes Ronan back and there is a bunch of yelling and swinging.

Just as Ronan punches one of the kids, a conservation officer who patrols the beaches arrives. "Hey! Knock that off!" he says as he wades into the water and pulls the kids apart.

The two boys, one of them with a bloody nose, point at Ronan and tell the officer that Ronan started it.

"*Did* you?" the officer asks him.

"Yes, I did! But they were going to pull one of his legs off just for fun. Who *does* that?"

"Ha!" says the taller one with a bloody nose. "He says the crab is a *his*. What a freak!"

The smaller boy yells, "And who hits someone for just picking up a horseshoe crab?"

"You weren't just picking him *up*. You were going to *hurt* him!" Ronan yells back.

The kid points to our clamming rakes. "You're here clamming. *What's* the difference?"

"Actually, there *is* a difference," the officer says. "You're not allowed to harvest horseshoe crabs here. It's against the law."

Ronan and the boys look at each other like they'd keep fighting if they could.

The officer gives the bloody-nosed kid some paper towels, telling him he'll be okay now that the bleeding has stopped. Then he checks our clamming permits. Finally, the officer takes out his phone, saying he'll have to call the police. That Ronan can't just hit someone in the face because he doesn't like what they're doing.

The Yarmouth police take two minutes to show up. They ask Ronan a bunch of questions and call his dad. Then they put Ronan in the back of the police car.

It makes me feel terrible to see Ronan taken away like that. Especially when the other two boys are watching and laughing.

Ronan shouldn't have done what he did. But he loves sea animals so much that I can understand how seeing the boys' cruelty, after getting that letter from his mom, was like lighting the fuse on a firecracker.

Chapter 34

CHATHAM PEER

As soon as my eyes open the next morning, I think of Ronan. Worried about what's happened. I wish I could call him, but their only phone is his dad's cell.

Grammy is yelling up the stairs to me, saying it's Lobster Roll Sunday, which is a holiday that Henry made up once where we all go to Chatham Pier for lobster rolls. It's not a fancy place, but it's the best spot on all of the Cape—and it's on the pier where the *Reel* is moored.

Just as Henry, Esme, Ruby, Olive, Grammy, and I are ready to pile into Esme's van for the drive, Ruby tells Henry she needs to go to the bathroom, so he takes her back inside. While they're inside, I hear Grammy tell Esme that maybe Ruby needs glasses. That makes sense—I think about the ways she trips on things and reaches for spots on the floor thinking they're objects.

I volunteer to sit in the wayback, hoping that I won't

have to do much talking. When Ruby tumbles into the seat next to me, I'm not exactly thrilled. But after she's buckled in, she puts her hands on both sides of my face and says, "You are sad."

"Yeah," I answer. "I am."

Ruby rests the side of her face against my arm, and her hand pats me slowly. "I'm sorry," she says. Just like her mom would do.

Henry glances back, and I can tell he has questions.

When we get to the pier, Ruby makes a run for the upper deck overlooking the boats coming in. Henry follows her and scoops her up. Looking over Chatham Harbor, Ruby squeals, "The *REEL*, Daddy! The *REEL*!" pointing at the only multicolored boat in the harbor.

"That's right, spitfire. That's right."

I walk down the stairs, drawing my hand lightly along a railing to avoid slivers, and walk out to the end of the pier. It's my favorite spot. When you stand on the edge, you can't see anything but water and sandbars and sky.

I stand, but not close to the edge. I close my eyes and smell the boat motors. Along with skunks, it's one of my favorite smells. I hear the fishermen yelling to each other and the sounds of heavy ropes hitting decks, chain pulleys lifting fish hauls onto the steel ramps, and the loud thud of a few thousand pounds of fish hitting the bottom of a cardboard box lined in plastic and ice.

I can tell the approaching footsteps are Henry's. He stands next to me and stays quiet for a few moments before clearing his throat and asking, "So what's going on?"

My first thought is to say that nothing is wrong, but the truth is that I want to tell him. I worry, though, that Ronan will be upset if I tell anyone.

"Well," I say, "you know how Grammy says that you don't go off telling people other people's business, acting like it's yours just because you know about it? You let people tell their own stories?"

"Yeah," he says, laughing. "I've heard her say that."

"Well, it's kind of like that. Not my story to tell . . . but . . ."

He tips his head to the side. "Is it Ronan?"

I nod.

He looks concerned. "Is he okay?"

"I . . . I'm not sure."

"Well, I don't know that telling me is gossip, honey. If Ronan needs help, I may be able to do something."

And so I tell him. The whole story and the whole truth. About how I thought his mom was dead but then she wrote him a letter and then he punched kids that he didn't even know and ended up in a police car. "Now," I say, "I don't know what's happened."

Henry scratches the back of his head and then smooths

out his hair from his forehead to the back. That's what Henry does when he's worried. "Well, maybe we'll go over there this evening. Check on things."

"Really?" I ask.

"Yeah." He takes a long breath. "Before I first took Ronan out on the *Reel*, his dad called me to introduce himself. And we realized that we know each other. Or we did. I knew Sherman Gale—or Gusty, as he goes by now—a long time ago. Back in the day we were both pretty foolish, and he had some trouble with using his fists instead of his words. So we'll lend some support to both of them."

Now I'm even more worried than I was before.

Chapter 35

WHO YOU GONNA BE?

Ronan opens the door when Henry knocks. "Hey there, Ronan. We came by to see how you're making out with things."

Ronan glares at me and doesn't say a word.

"Your dad home?" Henry asks.

Just then, Gusty comes out of the kitchen. "Ronan? Where are you going?" he says. Then he sees us. He stares at Henry long and hard, and I am frightened.

"May we come in?" Henry asks, and Ronan glances back at his father.

Gusty looks down at himself, his shoes covered in grass clippings. "You can come in, I s'pose," he says, "but we're not really set up for company."

Henry steps inside. "Nice place," he says.

"It's all right. Temporary housing for the position. I'm

looking for a permanent place for us to move to after the summer."

I can tell by the way Ronan's eyes widen that he didn't know they were going to have to move.

Henry extends his hand to Ronan's dad, but Gusty doesn't reach back—he just locks eyes with Henry and says, "It's been a long time."

"It has," Henry says. "A lot of water under the bridge since then." Henry looks at Ronan and then back at Gusty. "You have a fine boy here, Sherman. A really good kid. Smart. Tough. A good heart. Just like his father."

Gusty's head drops a bit, and he finally reaches for Henry's hand. And their shake is a long one. They finally let go, and Henry clears his throat as he turns to Ronan. He extends his hand again, and Ronan takes it. "How are you doing, Ronan?"

Ronan shrugs.

"Yeah," Henry begins. "I know about what happened at the beach. That's actually why I'm here."

Wait. What is he *doing*?

Gusty motions toward the couch to offer us seats. He scrambles to clear the pillows and blankets piled up on it. I look around and notice there is only one bedroom. Ronan must sleep on the couch.

"Thank you, Sherman," Henry says.

"Please call me Gusty. I haven't gone by Sherman in years." He nods at me and smiles. "Delsie there is awfully fond of my name." Gusty extends his hand to me, and we shake. "How've you been, Delsie? I appreciate how good you and your grandmother have been to my Ronan. This whole being-a-dad thing is new to me. Took me a while to find my sea legs. But we're doing all right now, Ronan and me."

This makes me smile and makes Ronan look at his father as if he can't believe what he's hearing.

"So," Henry says, turning to Ronan and me, "can you guys give us a few minutes?"

"Sure. C'mon," Ronan says, walking away. I follow. He pushes open a door off of the kitchen that leads into a bedroom with a New England Patriots poster and two shark posters. Ronan's jacket is on the bed. A baseball hat is on the side table.

"You have your own room?" I ask. "When I saw the stuff on the couch, I figured that was your bed."

"Naw, my dad had this done for me when I got here. I mean, it's just a bed and a couple of posters, but it's cool he gave me the room."

"Yeah, that *was* cool."

He turns toward me. "So you told Henry? I wish you hadn't done that."

"I'm sorry."

"It doesn't matter, I guess." He takes the hat from the side table and plays with the buckle on the back.

"So what happened when the police brought you home?"

"Well, for one, Brandy and Tressa were here to see it. Tressa was delightful."

I hadn't even thought about them. Which surprises me.

"My dad was . . . well, not happy. But he wasn't nearly as mad as I thought he would be. He said to stay put and then left to go fix something on the steps down at the beach. He came back later, reheated some of the stuff he calls his famous Portuguese seafood stew." He leans forward. "You know, I don't really like seafood. But he says his mom used to make it, so I try to eat it. So I have a grammy, too." He smiles. "But dad calls her my avó. That's Grammy in Portuguese."

"That's cool, Ronan. I hope I can meet your grammy . . . your avó . . . someday."

"Yeah. Me too. And guess what else? It turns out that the Portuguese shark is the deepest-living shark on earth. I love that. I think that's really cool."

"Me too, Ronan. That is cool."

He nods.

"So, you didn't get in trouble after the fight at the beach?"

"No. After stew, we just watched TV. My dad didn't say anything. Not *anything*. Except to tell me to brush my teeth."

Henry calls us into the living room then, and when we sit down, he and Gusty look more relaxed.

"I wanted to speak with both of you, but I wanted Gusty to hear as well," Henry says.

Ronan answers okay, but I'm too busy wondering what the heck is going on.

"I know you've had a tough time," Henry begins, looking at Ronan. "And how you came to be on the Cape. Anyone would be upset with what you've been through. But, selfishly, I'm glad you're here. You've been a good friend to Delsie. And *I'm* happy to know you."

"Thanks," Ronan mumbles.

Henry leans forward. "I'm here because I wanted to tell you a story. About myself."

"Okay."

"So, when I was eighteen, some friends and I were hanging down on Sea Street Beach, and someone suggested we go do some bad things. Things that were against the law."

"But you didn't go, right?" I ask.

"Well, Delsie, I *did* go. I knew it was wrong, and I knew it was stupid, but I went anyway. Because I'd had a terrible day and I had just graduated high school and didn't know what I was going to do. And I wasn't getting along well in the world. I was really struggling."

"What did you do?"

"We broke into a bunch of houses. Took people's things. Bad stuff. Things I would never do now."

"Wait," I say, feeling a bit dizzy. "*You* broke into people's houses?"

"I did, Delsie. I'm not proud of it, but as I said, I would never do that now." He turns to Ronan. "So for that I went to jail, Ronan. I took things that didn't belong to me. I stood by while a friend fought with a homeowner. I fled the scene and didn't call an ambulance when I should have. I went to jail for two years, and I was lucky it wasn't longer."

I feel awful.

Henry turns to me. "I've always told you about the little voice, right, Delsie?"

"Yeah," I say. "The little voice. I think of that all the time. It tells you you're about to do something dumb."

"That's right. I heard the voice that night and ignored it. And I paid for it."

Ronan turns to his father. "Were you there, too? You said you used to know each other."

Gusty draws in a deep breath and holds it. But Henry answers first. "Yes, Ronan. Your dad was there on the beach that night. But when we said we were going to do what we were going to do, he told us we were idiots. And he was right. Your dad was the *only* one who didn't go that night."

Ronan stares at his dad. Stares at him the way a person looks when a terrible storm has finally ended.

"So, in prison," Henry continues, "I had two years to think about what happened."

"That must have been awful," Ronan says. "A great white shark can't survive in captivity. Most die after a few days. They won't eat. They ram their heads into the walls of the tank."

"That makes sense," Henry says. "A strong animal like that. It's pretty awful to be locked up. So I had two years to decide what kind of life I was going to have when I got out. And getting out was not easy. People looked at me different. Treated me different. I had to tell people I'd been inside when I applied for jobs. It was hard to get someone to give me a chance. I was at the end of my rope. I even remember wondering if it wouldn't be easier to go back to jail."

He looks me right in the eye. "But it was your papa Joseph, Delsie. *He* was the one who told me a man is not made by his mistakes. He's made by what he does about them."

Henry stares at the floor and shakes his head. "And boy, did I work hard on his boat for him. Morning, noon, and night. I wanted him to respect me the way I respected him, but I knew I had to earn it. And I did."

He turns to Ronan. "So you made a mistake out of anger. But that doesn't mean that's who you are. Character is made or broken by patterns of behavior. Not one mistake."

"But I've made a lot of mistakes."

"Ronan," Gusty says. "I understand. I had a temper, too, but I learned that it takes *more* strength to control yourself than to fight."

Henry nods. "And I know you know a lot about sharks, Ronan, so I bet you know that a shark that doesn't keep moving forward can't survive."

Now Henry puts a hand on Ronan's shoulder. "I'm going to take a leap here and say that I think you've been through some hard stuff. I understand what that's like for a kid," Henry says. "I get that it leaves you feeling lost and wondering how you fit into the world."

Ronan nods.

"Some people aren't dealt easy hands, and it isn't fair. But I think if you play a difficult hand with courage and compassion, you end up stronger. It's hard, and I know there are times when the world beats you down and you feel like that's the only way it'll ever be."

Ronan lifts his head to look at Henry. "Yeah. It does feel that way."

"But the thing is, Ronan . . . the thing you really have to ask yourself is . . . are you going to live your life as a victim? Or a survivor?"

Chapter 36

BOOTS

Grammy's voice has a happy, ringing sound to it, like a buzzer on a game show. "C'mon, baby girl. I have a surprise in store for you."

"Is this like when you told me there was a surprise and we shopped for a rake? I mean, it *was* a surprise . . . but not a good one. And you know how I *love* surprises—"

Her belly laugh makes me laugh, too.

"What is the thing you've been begging and badgering me for all these years? Leaving notes around the house to remind me. In my shoes, in the sugar bowl."

I whip around to look at her. "Seriously? For real?"

"For real." She shakes her head. "Here I was trying to turn on my *Wheel of Fortune*, and the remote wouldn't work. So I open up the battery door, and what do I find? Another note about that kitten you have to have. It made me laugh so hard, I checked the *Cape Cod Times* and found an ad. Free kittens. I already stopped and got the basics, like litter and food, and I already spoke to the woman. She's waiting for us."

Grammy just kept talking about the lady with the kittens, but I think my brain couldn't listen anymore. All it could do was jump up and down. All I could do was imagine having my own kitten. Finally.

"Delsie?"

"Huh?"

"One condition. There's one condition. Well, besides your promise to take care of the critter. I *know* you'll do that."

"Anything! I'll do *anything*."

"I'm going to need my batteries back."

I smile.

• • •

I push the car door open and run to the small yellow house's front porch, ringing the bell before Grammy is even out of the car. She is coming up behind me as the front door swings open and a woman stands there, smiling.

"Hello there!" Grammy calls as she grabs the railing and pulls herself up the stairs. "We talked on the phone about the sweet kittens you have."

"Oh yes. Of course." She steps back and waves us into a house that smells like flowers. The woman can't stop staring at my bare feet. I hadn't noticed before how dirty they are.

"Won't you follow me? The kittens are back here." We walk around a corner, and she swings a bathroom door open. There are three kittens in a pile. Two are sleeping, and one is playing with its own tail.

"Grammy!" I say. "Can we take all three?"

"Oh, goodness no. We will *not* be taking three."

"Can I pick one up?" I ask.

The lady nods.

I scoop up the one playing with his tail. He is pure white with four black feet, and it makes me laugh. "I'll name him Boots! Look at his feet, Grammy." His fur is so soft that I can hardly even feel it as I pet him. I'm in love.

I walk through the doorway, holding the kitten against my chest. He plays with the string on my sweatshirt. My finger scratches under his chin and he purrs. I never knew that a purring cat feels like a mini version of Henry's generator. It makes me laugh again.

Grammy and the lady talk a bit about the weather and cats. Grammy starts talking about our car and how she prays every time she slides in but tells the lady not to worry. If the car won't start in the driveway, we have AAA.

The woman's phone dings, and she checks her screen. "I'm sorry. Will you excuse me for a moment?" she tells us, and she heads into the kitchen.

I hear loud whispering, and in a few moments, the woman is back.

Henry talks about wheels turning while people think on things—and this woman is thinking so hard right now, I can almost hear the gears. The little voice tells me that we should go.

"Well," Grammy says. "Thank you for the kitten. We'll be getting on our way."

I take two steps and then I hear the woman sigh. A sigh is never a good thing. Never. "I'm so sorry," she says. "I just can't."

"Can't what?" asks Grammy.

"I just can't let you have the cat. I just don't feel . . . like it's the right thing to do."

Wait. *What?*

"I really am sorry. I just don't see this as a good match." Then she reaches out and takes hold of the kitten.

"No!" I say, tightening my grip as the cat's claws hold the strings on my sweatshirt. As if he doesn't want to leave me, either. "Please don't take Boots. He's supposed to be mine. Please don't."

As she pulls the kitten away, I expect Grammy to say something, but she doesn't.

"I really am very sorry," the woman says, holding the kitten with one arm while reaching out with the other to grab the doorknob, giving us the sign to leave. The door closes gently behind us. But all I feel is a hard slam.

Grammy doesn't say a prayer, but the car starts anyway.

The rumbling of the engine reminds me of the purring kitten, but I swallow my tears to protect Grammy. As she puts the car into reverse, I look back up at the house, and standing there on the porch, with her arms folded and that smug smile, is Tressa.

Chapter 37

EGGS AND POTATOES

I hand Ronan a Strong Shoulder jar half filled with lemonade. "Here. There wasn't much left, so I split it between us."

"Thanks," he says, taking a drink.

I sit on the bench next to him, shaking my jar a bit to hear the clinking of the ice cubes. Noticing that the jar is half full. "So." I hold up my jar and look at the sun through lemonade. "Would you say that this jar is half empty or half full?"

He stares and thinks for a few seconds. "Neither. The jar is just twice as big as it needs to be."

"That wasn't a choice." I laugh.

"Of *course* it was."

I shake the jar to clink the cubes again. The jar is cold and wet and slippery, so it falls away from me. I reach, my fingers scrambling to catch it before it hits the patio. Glass smashes on the cement.

I move forward, but Ronan is already off the bench. "No! You stay. You have bare feet."

Oh yeah.

He picks up the big pieces of glass and stacks them in a pile. A little tower of broken glass.

I think of the day I broke the candy-covered frame with my mother's picture in it. And I think of Grammy's puzzles, all broken up until someone puts them together.

"Ronan?" I ask.

"Yeah?" he asks, picking up pieces of smaller glass caught in the grass that grows up through the cracks in the cement.

"Do you think a person can break like a jar does? Can a person be hit so hard by something that they . . . that they break?"

"Naw. A body is too soft to shatter into pieces."

"No, not break into pieces. I mean like the insides of a person."

"You mean like appendicitis or something?"

"No," I say, my voice trailing off. "Not like that. That's not what I mean . . ."

He stands watching me. His head tips to the side. "What are you *talking* about, Delsie?"

My mouth doesn't want to say the words.

He waits.

I stare him dead in the eyes. "Do you think we're broken?"

His eyebrows scrunch up. "What do you mean . . . *broken*?"

"I mean . . . *broken*. Why would my mother just leave me? And why would your mom send you away? There must be something wrong with us."

"No. Don't say that. That isn't right."

"Yeah, but—"

"And besides," he interrupts, stepping forward, "even when something is broken, you can fix it."

I shake my head. "I mean, you can fix a dishwasher, but not everything can be fixed." I point at the pile of glass he's made on the cement. "We can't put that jar back together."

"Yeah, well . . . maybe you're right about that . . . but, well, we can make sure we don't step on it."

I think about what that means. Maybe I've been stepping where I shouldn't lately. When I look back up at Ronan, he has stuffed his hands in his pockets and he's looking up at the trees.

"Be the egg," he says, with a single nod.

"Be the egg?" I ask. "Is that what you said?"

"Yeah. Be the egg. Not the potato."

"Ronan? Why are you saying that? Is it a riddle?"

Ronan's face turns red. "Delsie. I try so hard not to . . ."

He can't finish.

I want to say something to him, but I still don't know what he's talking about.

"We didn't leave them. They left us. They did the leaving, right? That wasn't *our* fault."

"Yeah . . ." I agree.

"So how can *we* be broken because of something someone *else* has done?"

I *know* that's true. But I have to try to *feel* that it's true. I can't take my eyes off the broken glass on the ground.

"Why were you talking about eggs and potatoes?" I ask.

"Because I want you to know that we're both eggs, Delsie. Not potatoes."

"Why are we eggs and not potatoes?"

"Think of what happens to each when you put them in boiling water."

I smile, but his face makes me sad. It's like inside he is begging for me to agree. He needs me to agree.

"Well, I'd rather be hard-boiled like an egg than a smooshy potato mess, but . . ." Staring at the glass pieces, I think about Esme and the Strong Shoulder jars. "I don't know, Ronan. I think maybe we're more like tea bags. In hot water, we just get stronger and stronger."

A smile spreads across Ronan's face. And then we both laugh. We both laugh so hard, it almost feels like crying.

Chapter 38

NOW WE'RE COOKIN'

Henry lugs out the half barrel for another neighborhood cookout. Ruby is dragging an empty cooler, and Esme is following her with bags of ice.

"Ruby," I ask, "why are you always covered in Band-Aids?"

"I like how they smell."

"How they smell?"

"Yeah, they smell all Band-Aidy. I like them. And I like how people act about them."

"What do you mean?"

"When people see them, they act all nice, asking me how I hurt myself and if I'm okay, and I like it."

I smile at her logic. "And are you okay, Ruby? Are people being nice to you?"

"Everyone but Olive." Ruby frowns. "Olive says I'm clumsy and probably trip over my own shadow."

I put my arm around Ruby and pull her close. I think of the elephants that Esme told me about and how Ruby is sort of like my little sister. I'm going to be extra good to her.

Grammy drives up, and Ronan is in her car. "Look what I found on the road." Grammy laughs as she gets out of the car. "I told him it was cookout night and he should come over."

"Hey, everyone. What's for dinner? Not that it matters." He smiles.

"Crab cakes," I say.

He makes a face, and I laugh, telling him that I'm kidding.

Henry has got some of Esme's island music playing and uses his root beer bottle as a microphone to sing to us while he cooks.

Soon, Olive trudges across the neighborhood, pine needles flying, looking all Olive-like. But she has a white box in her hands. What could she be carrying?

She steps up to Ruby, and I join them, feeling a bit worried; Olive lets some pretty awful things fly when she talks to her.

Esme is also nearby, keeping an eye out.

Olive, clutching the box, looks up at both Esme and me. "What? Is this a committee? I just wanted to talk to Ruby for a minute."

"Go ahead," Esme says.

Olive's expression looks like she just stepped on a tack. "Here," she says, pushing the ratty box toward Ruby. "This is yours."

Esme looks nervous, but lets Ruby open it. What's inside is too beautiful for such a box.

"Oooooooh," Ruby says, pulling out a dress. It's a quilt of many different squares of fabric in all colors of purple with some red and orange sprinkled in. I've never seen anything like it. It seems to glow. Underneath there is another dress. Identical but small. Like it's for a doll.

Ruby looks up, wide-eyed but sad. "They aren't mine."

Olive sighs. "Well, of *course* they are, child. You've been prattling on for months that you wanted that Melody doll and matching outfits. I couldn't manage the expensive doll, but I thought the dress could be worn by another of your dolls."

Ruby's happy squeal hits a note I swear could shatter glass.

Olive looks nervous.

Esme speaks slowly. "So . . . you *bought* these somewhere?"

"No. I couldn't do *that*. I made them. Been working on them since March ninth. My sewing machine died, so I had to stitch them by hand."

"*Wait*. You *made* these? By *hand*?"

Olive stands like a statue.

"Oh my!" Esme says. "I don't know what to say, Olive. They're gorgeous!"

"W-well," Olive sputters. "You don't need to say . . . *anything*."

She spins and takes a step away and then turns back. She speaks fast. "They're purple because you and your momma love that color. Although I don't know why. And look." She points to a quilt square. "I searched for a fabric with red wagons on it. There's some fish on there for your father. And some silly bright lizards to match the ones on your house. You'll have to look for the other things yourself. So that's that."

And she spins and stomps away the same way she came. Man, just when I thought Olive couldn't possibly surprise me any more. Isn't it strange how she can be so sharp and yet so soft, too?

Chapter 39

RUNAWAY

I'm waiting in the parking lot for Grammy to finish her last room when I see the two people I hoped I wouldn't run into. Brandy and Tressa. Weird, though. They are walking a dog. One of those little puffball dogs that some ladies carry in big bags over their shoulders.

I decide I will not run off. I'm going to hold my ground and talk to them if they talk to me and hold it together no matter what Tressa does.

And no matter what Brandy doesn't do.

"Hello, Delsie," Tressa says, with her fake smile. "Whatcha doing?"

I hold her eyes. "Waiting for Grammy. So, whose dog?" I ask.

"Mrs. Devine in building three."

I squat and scratch its head. "It's cute."

"I don't know about that—but it's worth ten dollars to walk him," Tressa says. She bends over and tucks the handle of the leash under a big rock.

There's an awkward silence until we hear a loud bark from a dog in a car pulling out across the street. The dog that Tressa is supposed to be watching goes running, pulling the leash out from under the rock and darting across the street. He's faster than he looks. And he's trying his best to catch the car with his furry friend.

"No!" Tressa yells, running after the dog. Brandy follows and so do I.

A car swerves to miss the furry runner. Tressa squeals, slowing down. Brandy, too.

"Oh no! What am I going to do? That woman will kill me!" I hear Tressa say as I whiz past. My bare feet slip a bit in the loose sand on the side of the road.

I see the dog up ahead, realizing he will not catch the car. He spins on the side of the road, his leash winding around his feet. And I am approaching super fast. When he sees me, he takes off again, and I am grateful that he's a dog with short legs rather than long ones.

If I just grab the leash, I could hurt his neck, so I run alongside of him, bend over, and pick up the leash. However, trying to save the dog, I stumble. I never stumble, but I do now. My elbows are the first to hit the ground, followed by my knees, but I do keep hold of the leash.

As I lie on the side of the road, the dog licks my face, and I mumble, "If you like me that much, you could have just sat and waited for me." And something about it makes me think of the old Brandy. I really do miss her. I miss who she used to be.

A car pulls over as I stand up. A woman jumps out. "Oh my goodness! Are you okay?" She bends over and looks at my knees and breathes in through her closed teeth. "Oh, I'm so sorry. I think I have Band-Aids in the car."

I'd actually like to sit by the road and have this complete stranger help me with my cuts. But I do what I'm supposed to do. I stand up straight and say, "It doesn't hurt. But thank you."

"But . . ." she begins.

I try not to wince. "I have to get back to my mom and dad on the beach. They'll be worried," I say.

And as I walk back, I wonder why I told her that I had to get back to pretend parents when I have a perfectly good, real grammy who will clean my cuts and cover me with Band-Aids. I wish I hadn't said it now.

• • •

Tressa and Brandy are on the swings when I get back with the dog.

Tressa runs over. When she drops to her knees to tell the dog how bad he is, she looks right into my bloody knees. When she stands, I expect a mean comment. The kind Olive would give Ruby when she has Band-Aids.

But she doesn't say something mean. "Thank you. I mean, thanks, Delsie."

I'm shocked. "You're welcome."

Then she holds out the ten-dollar bill. "Here. This is the money I got for walking the dog."

"It's okay. I don't need that. But thanks anyway."

She looks like Tressa again. "I'm not giving it to you to be nice. You got the dog back, so I'm giving you the money. I just don't want to owe you anything."

That makes sense. "Believe me. You don't owe me *any-thing*," I say as I turn to walk away. And I mean every word.

Chapter 40

THE FEELING OF BEING ROBBED

Ronan and I run up the drive into my little neighborhood; we slow to a jog and then a walk. I bend over and rest my hands on my knees, trying to catch my breath. And then I hear voices I don't recognize. And I see blue and red lights flashing across the front of Olive's house. "What's going on?" I mumble.

I sprint down the drive and around the corner, with Ronan on my heels. There is a police car in front of our house. I feel like I'm going to throw up. Is something wrong with Grammy?

As we get closer, I hear Grammy's voice. A bit of a wail and a cry wrapped around each other. And I am relieved she's making noise. Then I'm afraid again.

"Who would *do* such a thing?" she asks the police officer.

"Our most treasured possessions. I just don't understand people."

"Yes, ma'am. I am sorry for your losses. We will do our best to recover your things. We'll check local pawnshops and the like. If you think of anything else, please let us know."

"Oh, Delsie, baby. We've been robbed."

"*What?*" I begin to think of the things that could be gone that we'll miss. The television, for one. I don't know how Grammy will get by without that.

"Grammy, what did they take? The TV?"

"No, no. They left that. Too hard to carry, I suppose. They took very dear things, though, like my Joseph's pocket watch."

"Oh no . . ." I say, my voice trailing off.

"And—I'm so sorry, Delsie—they took some of your mother's things. Jewelry. Pins. Old coins. Lots of stuff that wouldn't mean a hill of beans to other people but us."

Uh-oh, I think, glancing at the police officer. What have I done?

"They even took my sweet mother's diamond ring, which I'd given to your mom. It's a tiny stone, but it was big to me for what it meant to me to have it."

What? That was actually a *diamond*? And I buried it in the backyard? Oh boy . . .

"Um . . ." I say. "Grammy?"

"Yes, honey bunch?"

"We weren't robbed."

"Now, baby, I know it's hard to accept, and I—"

I interrupt. "No, Grammy. Listen. I'm . . . I'm so sorry! I didn't even think—"

The police officer steps forward. "Do you know who took the items, miss?"

I turn. "Yes. It was *me*."

Grammy is on her feet. "You? That doesn't make sense. Why in tarnation would you take things that already belong to you?"

"I'm sorry, Grammy. I just wanted to protect them. I was afraid you would sell them if we needed money. And I have lost so much. Well, I wanted those things from my mom and Papa to remind me of them. Just to have. Something of theirs that is . . . just mine . . . which is terrible, I know. I'm so sorry."

She looks relieved but embarrassed.

"Grammy, I'd never hurt our stuff. It wasn't like that. I just wanted to keep everything safe."

Grammy laughs, which shocks me. "Well, that's good news, I guess."

"*Good* news?" Ronan asks.

"Well, the child cares about her family. I can't slight her for that."

I am so relieved.

The officer has folded his pad and put it in his pocket. "Well, I guess I'll head out, then. Seems that everything is in order."

"Thank you, Officer," Grammy says. "I'm so sorry to have called you out here for nothing."

"No problem, ma'am." And he is gone.

I stand there. Waiting for her question that I'm sure is coming. "So where are our things, then? In your room?"

"Oh . . . um . . . no."

"Well, where, then?"

"I buried it all in a jar in the backyard."

"A *jar* . . . in the *yard*?"

"I know," I say. "It seemed like a good idea at the time." And it all comes out of me like water over a clogged gutter. "You say that you can't look at their things because it makes you too sad to remember and I know that we need money for the car and the furnace that spews the soot but I was so afraid that you would sell their things and I just . . . I just *couldn't* let go of the few things we have left of theirs. And I feel terrible, Grammy. I'm so sorry. I know the things hurt you. But for me, I guess that I feel different than you when I see Papa's things. Or even my momma's things, even though I don't know her. Holding the things Papa Joseph loved makes me miss him but also happy that he was my papa Joseph."

Grammy leans forward and comes to me. She cradles my

222

face in her hands and locks eyes with me. Her blue eyes, the color of faded denim, shine. "Of *course* you feel that way. Because you have a loving heart. And . . . well . . . I guess the truth of it is that you are much braver than your ole grammy."

And when she kisses the top of my head and I rest my cheek on her soft shoulder, I finally feel like I can sit with the sad and the happy all at the same time.

And share it with Grammy.

Chapter 41

FELINE KINDER

Grammy is the best. She promised me that we won't sell anything that was in the Strong Shoulder jar, *and* she gave me my mother's whale ring to keep.

As I wash the dirt from the jar, I think about how, like a seed in the ground, burying made things grow. But not in a good way. Just like how *not* talking about things can make stuff feel like a bigger problem, and even more confusing.

I'm drying the jar when the doorbell rings.

Since it's pretty much understood that if the place isn't burning down, I get the door if Grammy is watching television, I swing open the door. It's Tressa, looking at our house the same way she did the first time. Same pink lips all bunched together like a giant wad of bubble gum.

The difference is that I don't care what she thinks anymore.

She acts like she's a secret agent, glancing from side to side, leaning away from the glow of our porch light, and asking in a loud whisper, "Can I talk to you for a second? Outside, I mean?"

I step outside slowly.

She assumed I'd follow. Why not? She's Tressa. She could probably herd bedbugs. She walks around the corner toward the backyard, and I follow her. I'm curious.

Then she turns around. "Hey. Why did you do that with the dog?" she asks.

"Because."

"That isn't an answer."

"I wanted to save the dog," I say. "I didn't do it for you or even the lady who owns the dog. I wanted to save the dog."

She stares at the Band-Aids on my knees. Enough Band-Aids to make Ruby jealous.

"Yeah, well, for the record, the last thing I want is to feel like I owe you anything."

"I already told you that you don't owe me anything. Nada. Zilch."

Tressa raises an eyebrow at me. "I don't understand. Why wouldn't you take the money?"

"You know," I say, "you *could* just say thank you."

She folds her arms. "Well, as you said, you did it for the dog. Not me."

"Yeah. I did."

"Okay, then," she says. "I just want to make sure that we're even."

I think about telling her that we will never be even, as in *the same*, but I know she wouldn't understand and she'd want to argue. I don't want to win a fight with her. I just want her to go so I can be happy again.

"Fine," I say, and she turns to go. *Finally*.

She's almost out of sight, then stops, turns back, and says, "Check the back stoop."

"Huh?"

"There's something on the back stoop," she repeats before walking away.

Oh, that's great. The first thing I think of is one of those metal bear traps that snap on your ankle if you step on it.

I look carefully at the ground with each step, remembering that she knows I always have bare feet. Does she want me to end up with nails in my feet?

I hear a high squeak as I approach the stoop. And scratching, too. All coming from a cardboard box. I leap five feet in one step and carefully open the top.

I never thought I'd be one of those people who cry at weddings and stuff. It made no sense to me to cry when you're happy—but I understand it now. In the darkening light, I can see a ball of bright white fur. Then I make out the pink nose. I scoop up my kitten—my very own kitten—into my arms. "It's you, Boots!" I squeal.

Finally. Someone I've lost that I've gotten back.

Chapter 42

TO REVEAL A SECRET

Running down the wooden steps at Seaside, I see Ronan at the water's edge. It reminds me of the day I first saw him. Standing with his feet in the surf in the middle of a lightning storm.

That first day I saw him, I never would have thought we could be friends. Thinking about how wrong I was makes me stop in my tracks for a second and stare at him.

Then I run toward him and leap into the air. I land right next to him. "Hey, what's up?"

He looks at me with such a smile. A smile I've never seen on him. Like his whole body is contributing.

"*What?*" I ask.

"*What?*" he answers back.

"Don't give me that. You look like you won the lottery or something."

"*Huh.* Maybe . . . maybe I did. Or I will."

"Are you going to *tell* me?"

"Not yet. I can't."

I sigh. I refuse to beg him. "*Fine*, then."

He turns away as if he's trying to hide his smile. And my insides begin to argue. One side saying it reminds me of Tressa and Brandy and how they'd make a joke of me. And the other part telling me that Ronan would never do that. I know he'd never do that. He isn't someone to just watch me eat a sandwich. But I don't like not knowing what is going on.

He must be able to tell it bothers me. "It's a surprise."

"Oh no. I hate surprises," I blurt out. "That's one of the reasons I love my Weather Channel. I like to know what's coming."

"But how can anyone hate surprises?"

"Well, not all surprises are good ones," I say, but then I think about my new kitten—finally, a nice surprise.

"Well," Ronan says, "you'll find out soon enough. I hope you'll like it." Then he tugs at my sleeve. "But come look at this!" He runs and I follow him. And I can't believe it.

It's not uncommon to find a lobster trap washed up on-shore, but to find a live lobster inside?

"How cool is that?" I say. "Henry will pay us for him, you know. Probably ten bucks."

"Wait a sec," he says. "First of all, I found him, so no way is anyone going to eat him. Look at him. He's *beautiful*." He bends over and points at the top of his shell. "There's even a tinge of blue there. See that?"

"Yeah. Delicious. Blue lobster and melted yellow butter. Mmmmm," I say to tease him, but crack up over his expression. "I know, I know. You're going to let him go, aren't you? I think I've seen this movie before."

"*Yeah*, I'm going to let him go. I'm not going to save him . . . and then *eat* him. That's like one of those horror movies that comes on in the middle of the night." Then he talks in a creepy voice. "Here. Let me save you. Oh, this butter I'm melting? Oh, that's nothing. That's for a giant piece of toast that they're bringing in with a helicopter."

My stomach hurts from laughing.

He breaks his way into the trap more easily than I would have figured and grabs the lobster, who starts waving his powerful claws around. "Ah! He's trying to get me! Oh my . . . No! Stop!"

I laugh. "They can't get you if you hold the body."

Ronan doesn't listen and rushes to the water, falling into a giant wave. It knocks him sideways and spins him around. His feet stick up through the top of the wave. If I weren't laughing so hard, I'd try to help him.

He comes out of the water looking a little dizzy. "Where is he? Where did he go?"

I point toward the open ocean. "That way, I guess."

"Aw, man." He rinses the sand from his face and hair.

"It's awful. I have the grace of a landslide. Flexibility of an earthquake."

I'm trying not to laugh again. I can't even count how many times I've been flipped over by a wave. "Happens to everyone. Are you okay? It looked like you were caught in a water tornado."

"I let him go. I meant to bring him out to deeper water."

"Well, he's safer in shallow water than out there," I say, pointing to the lobster traps. "Their most dangerous predators are people. If he's hungry for bait, he'll get caught again."

"Oh no," he groans.

"Ronan. You do know you're on Cape Cod, right? And . . ." I hesitate. "I mean, aren't you the son of a fisherman?"

"Yeah, I know." He rolls his eyes. "I told my father I was saving my money to buy lobsters at the grocery store. He was happy until I told him I was buying them to set them free. You should have seen his face."

"Was he mad?"

"Naw. He said I'd probably be a scientist one day. Save endangered species and stuff. He called me Dr. Gale all night. It was goofy. And cool."

I'm happy that Ronan's dad is nice to him.

"Ronan! Hey, Ronan!"

We turn around. His dad is yelling for him from the top of the stairs.

He breaks into that smile again. "Wait here. I'll be right back!"

I watch as he talks to his dad. Ronan pumps his fist like he just made a soccer goal. He jumps a bit and then runs toward me. Faster than I have ever seen him run.

This time he lands in front of me after a long leap into the air, and I want to laugh. He still looks like he lost a battle with a sandcastle.

"Guess what," he says, about to bust.

"*What?*" I ask, thinking I'm going to find out what the surprise is, hoping it's a good one.

"My dad just bought a hot dog bun."

I shake my head. "*That's* your surprise? Man, Ronan, if you're this excited about that, you must be having a bad week."

He laughs. "Not just *any* hot dog bun. The one near the smooshed-up pickles and vinegar-soaked cucumbers."

"Wait. *What?*"

His whole body laughs.

"Are you telling me . . . ?"

"Yup! We bought the abandoned house!"

Ronan and I jump up in the air like we're little kids. We can't stop laughing. I wonder how I could get so lucky. And I also think that there *is* such a thing as a good surprise.

Chapter 43

A LESSON FROM MOBY

The word Nantucket means "Faraway Land" in the Algonquian language. That makes sense—it feels like it takes forever to get there on Henry's boat.

"There's a lighthouse!" I yell over the motor as Henry, Ronan, and I cut through the water.

"Sure is! Brant Point Light!" Henry calls. "And on the other side of the island is my favorite—Sankaty Head Lighthouse. They've already moved that one back once because the bluffs are falling into the ocean at one to two feet a year. Scientists say Nantucket will disappear completely in about four hundred years. I'm going to leave in three hundred, as I don't want to see that."

Henry laughs louder than any of us. I've never known anyone who laughs so much at his own jokes.

We drop anchor at a place called Tuckernuck. There are

a few other boats and a bunch of people in the water, so I ask Henry if I can go in, too. He looks around. Takes out binoculars. "Well, I don't see any seals, which is good. Just stay between the boat and the land."

When I dive into the water, I go from sweltering hot to nice and cool. I swim underwater until I can't hold my breath anymore and rise to the surface.

Ronan stands on the side wall of Henry's boat, looking out at me as I tread water. All of a sudden, his face is covered in fear as he stares past me.

I turn and am unable to scream. Unable to move.

A gray fin is coming toward me. And whatever that fin belongs to is huge.

"Delsie!" Ronan is screaming. "Delsie!" And there is a splash. Ronan is in the water coming toward me. The fin is coming my way as well. My brain screams to swim, but I can't move.

Henry is yelling, too—something I can't understand over the splashing and the yelling and the fact that I am so terrified.

Ronan swims next to me. He has a buoy. Why?

"Ronan! Be careful!" I yell.

He faces the fin, looking like he's ready to fight.

I finally make out that Henry is yelling, "It's okay! It's okay!"

There is nothing okay about this.

We watch as the fin circles. The shark is wide and round. It's enormous.

Henry is yelling still. "It's a sunfish. It won't hurt you. It's a sunfish. It's okay. It won't hurt you."

Wait. What?

I turn and look again. Henry is cupping his hands around his mouth to be louder. "Look at the fin. Floppy on top. It's not a shark."

Ronan lets out a gasp, and so do I. We laugh with relief as the enormous, goofy-looking fish with the floppy fin circles us. Curious, I guess.

"I thought you knew everything about sharks!" I say.

"Well, I know a lot about sharks, but I don't know anything about sunfish! I thought the fin was weird, but I panicked just based on its size. It's huge!"

I point at the buoy in his hand. "What did you bring that for?"

"If you hit a great white in the eyes, it sends them off."

"But you love great whites," I tease him. "You would hit one for me?"

"Duh, what do you *think*?"

When we are back on the boat, Henry shakes his head. "You're an impressive kid, Ronan. You really are. But even you couldn't beat a great white."

"I was going to punch him in the eyes or the gills with the buoy. That stuns them. They'll swim away if you hit

235

them hard and in the right place. I've read all about it in books."

"Written by someone with no arms. Or *worse*."

"They're fighters," Ronan says.

"Yeah, and some fighters it's probably best not to mess with." Henry looks at me. "You know which animal in the ocean is a *real* fighter? And your mom's favorite, Delsie?" he says, pointing at the ring on my finger. "The sperm whale."

I touch the whale with my fingertip. "She liked them that much? *Why?*"

"Because they fought back when whalers harpooned them. Right in these very waters, actually. Back in the 1800s. Now, the other types of whales? Well, they'd die pretty conveniently once the harpooner stuck 'em. But the sperm whale . . . it crashed boats into toothpicks. Pulled boats across the sea at high speed bouncing over the waves. Men hanging on for their lives. They'd even pull the boats underwater. That was called the Nantucket sleigh ride. And it was deadly for men."

Henry stares off at the sky like he's figuring something out. "You know, Delsie, you have a lot in common with your mom. You laugh like her. The way you stand. But you have one big difference."

"We do?"

"She always waited for ships to come in, but you swim out to them."

"Huh?"

"She waited for things to come to her. You chase them down." He looks over at Ronan and back at me. "You're both like that, actually. It will be great to see what you two manage to make of yourselves. I can't wait."

Chapter 44

THE SUN WILL COME OUT

I just about flew across the neighborhood when Esme told me that she had a friend at the playhouse who had given her tickets for us all to see *Annie*. They even got a ticket for Ronan. When I told her how happy I was about that, Esme said, "Well, he's one of *us* now, isn't he?"

So when the big day arrives, Olive, Grammy, the Laskos, Ronan, and I all pile onto a bench in the back of the theater. I see Mrs. Fiester first. Then Brandy and Tressa follow. Brandy sees me and waves a little, and I wave back. They head up to the front of the theater and sit really close to the stage.

The play begins with "It's a Hard-Knock Life," and I think about how differently I feel about that song now than I did before. Papa Joseph used to say that if everyone put their troubles in the middle of the table, most would take their own back. I wasn't sure what he was talking about when I was younger, but now I get it—I don't think my life is *too* hard-knock after all.

But mostly, I sit up real straight so I can see as much as I can of Michael and Aimee.

Aimee is amazing as Annie. The audience loves her, and I'm so proud of her.

And Michael turned out to be a great Rooster. He acted like such a twit, I'm sure he made Madam Schofield proud.

At the end, I am the first to lead the standing ovation. I hoot and holler and yell Michael's and Aimee's names. Aimee looks for me in the audience, and when she finally sees me, she waves wildly.

When Ronan and I go to wait outside the stage door to see Aimee and Michael, Tressa and Brandy are there, too.

When Aimee arrives, I start yelling, "Miss Polloch! Miss Polloch! May I have your autograph!" I do the same for Michael.

Aimee unhooks the rope that everyone must wait behind and says, "C'mon, Delsie and Ronan! The director said I can take you backstage. I'll show you the costumes and stuff."

"Aimee. *Delsie*," Tressa yells. "Can we come, too?"

Before we can say anything, Michael steps forward.

"Aren't you the one who wrote on her back with sunscreen and treated her like trash all summer? Now you want a favor? I don't think so."

Tressa squints. Brandy stares at me. But not in an angry way. She looks sad, actually.

"It's okay, Michael," I say. "I don't care if they come if you and Aimee are okay with it."

"After everything they *did*?" he asks. "Are you *kidding* me?"

I shrug. "That stuff happened earlier in the summer. It just doesn't matter anymore," I say, feeling stronger. Knowing that I have real friends who have my back and will protect my feelings—people like Aimee, Michael, and Ronan—makes all the difference. Brandy and Tressa going backstage won't change any of that.

Michael's still not convinced.

"Besides," I say, "Tressa came to my house and gave me my kitten, Boots. And that made me pretty happy."

Brandy whips her head around. "*What?*" She turns to Tressa. "You *did*?"

Tressa shrugs. "Yeah. Whatever. Can we come or not? I didn't know this was going to be a committee."

"Why didn't you tell me?" Brandy asks her.

Tressa looks away. "It's not like I have to tell you *every*thing."

The look that falls over Brandy's face tells me that Tressa doesn't protect her feelings, either.

Watching Brandy, I realize this makes me wish I could have kept her from changing this summer. Kept her from doing all the things that she did. And didn't do. And then I think of my mom and wish I could keep her from doing the things she does. The things that made her leave and keep her away. It really is true that you can control other people about as easily as you can control the weather.

Aimee takes Michael by the shoulders and moves him over. "C'mon," she says. "Whoever is coming. C'mon." And with that, we all follow her up the stairs and into the playhouse.

Chapter 45

THE ONES WHO STAY

The costume room backstage in the playhouse is the coolest thing ever. Like the rest of the theater, it is wallpapered with old posters from shows throughout the history of the playhouse. It's filled with a mixture of gorgeous gowns and costumes from different time periods.

Aimee walks up to a door that says GERTRUDE LAWRENCE DRESSING ROOM and spins around. "This is my dressing room." She swings open the door, and there is a picture of a woman in one of those fancy dresses that is so big that it arrives a minute before the lady does. In front of the picture is a small shelf with a vase full of blue hydrangeas. "*That* is Gertrude Lawrence," Aimee tells us. "She died on opening night of *The King and I*. Now she haunts the Cape Playhouse. If there aren't fresh hydrangeas for opening night on that shelf, tragedy will occur."

"C'mon, you believe that?" Tressa says.

"It's *true*. Two directors have ignored the flowers, and on both nights, the show could not finish."

"What happened?" Ronan and Brandy both ask.

"The power went out one time. And some stuff fell on-stage the other time."

"Was someone hurt?" I ask.

"No. But the play couldn't finish."

Actors and actresses are scurrying about. There is a lot of calling of each other's names. And the smell of flowers. A lot of actresses have flowers. I look up at the bright lights shining down until a shadow falls upon me. It's Madam Schofield scurrying in, holding hydrangeas in her hand.

"Magnificent! You were magnificent! I always love it when a good actor makes *me* look good." Madam Schofield hands Aimee the flowers and exclaims, "These are for you! In the tradition of our beloved Gertrude Lawrence." She turns to Michael. "And you, sir. I had my doubts in the beginning. But you, Mr. Poole, gave a deep performance. Spectacular work."

Clearly, Aimee and Michael are as shocked as I am.

She spins and runs off.

Then, while Tressa acts like she's Aimee's new best friend, Ronan leans over and whispers in my ear, "I feel bad for Brandy. She reminds me of a pilot fish."

I give him a why kind of look.

"Because they live inside a shark's mouth and eat off of

the back of the shark's teeth. They're too small to get bitten. Except . . . Brandy clearly gets bitten."

He's right—and for a minute I feel sorry for her.

I walk over and stand next to Brandy. "Hey."

She tries to answer, but it gets stuck. She clears her throat and tries again. "Hey."

"You going back home soon?"

"Yeah. Tomorrow." She shifts her weight back and forth a bit before saying, "It was a weird summer."

"It was," I agree.

"Yeah," she says. "And I can't believe you hung around that *kid* all summer. *Ronan.*"

I look over at Ronan, who is searching the cracks in the floor, trying to retrieve something. "Well," I say, "I like him. Turns out he's a good friend. Someone I can count on, you know?"

She nods slightly but looks past me at Tressa, who sounds overly happy all of a sudden. "Aimee," Tressa gushes, "you should come to *my* house sometime this fall. I can take you to the theater district in Boston."

"Oh," Michael jumps in. "The wolf wants Little Red Riding Hood to visit."

Tressa glares at him while Aimee catches my eye and smiles. She comes over and links her arm with mine as we get ready to leave the playhouse. "That girl could use some good acting lessons," she says.

"For sure," I say, happy that Aimee can see through Tressa so easily.

"Madam Schofield told us that it isn't about *just* saying your lines," Aimee continues. "The most important thing is to pay attention to the *others* on the stage. To have a clue about what they are thinking. And respond to what they do and say."

That's good advice. And it's pretty clear Tressa doesn't bother about what anyone else is thinking. But Brandy used to. I wonder if she can ever go back to who she was.

Before we leave, I approach her. "Well, Brandy," I say. "Good luck this year."

"Yeah. You too, Dels."

As I turn away, I feel a twinge of sadness at Brandy's use of my old nickname, until I see Ronan grinning at me. He's holding up an old penny.

"Look!" he says. "I found this wheat penny in the boards. They're good luck, you know." Ronan holds it out to me. "Here. I want you to have it."

I take it from him, even though I know I don't need that penny. I'm already lucky.

• • •

That night, I crawl into bed, stare at the lucky penny, and think about all the things that make me lucky.

There's Ronan. But then again, having him as a friend isn't pure luck; it's because we gave each other a chance. And soon he's going to be my neighbor. I can't think of anything that's ever happened that has made me so happy. Ronan and his dad living right across from us. It's like a rainstorm after a drought—and I didn't even know a friendship like his was missing till I found it.

I'm lucky to have Aimee and Michael, too. And to not care that I don't have Brandy anymore.

And I've *always* been lucky to have Grammy. My mind flashes back to when I landed in the hospital in the fifth grade with a fever that wouldn't break.

I remember the nurse telling Grammy it was time to go home. That I would be sleeping and she could come back tomorrow.

I remember the panic that ran through me until she straightened her back and told that nurse, "There isn't anything on God's green earth that's gonna make me leave my Delsie."

The woman opened her mouth to say something else, but Grammy interrupted her. "And if you are going to tell me that you're calling security, well, take a look at me and ask yourself how many officers it's going to take to move me. You'll need the National Guard and a helicopter and a tank and maybe a bunch of horses. Because I'm not leaving my baby's side, no matter what you or anyone else says."

I think about those two words. *My baby.* Not *this* baby or *a* baby but *my* baby.

They let her stay, and we watched *Let's Make a Deal*. Grammy gave all kinds of advice, and we laughed about the man dressed like a cow in a tutu. I laugh to myself about Grammy making a fuss. And the expression on the nurse's face when Grammy talked about tanks and helicopters.

I know.

I know that I will wonder. I will always wonder what it would have been like to grow up with my mother. But I also know that, no matter what, I'd never trade my grammy and our life together for whatever is behind door number two.

Chapter 46

WHAT YOU SEE

There's a chill in the air, and a few fallen leaves dot the lawn at Seaside. Ronan has spent the morning helping his dad cover up all of the grills and move the lawn chairs into storage. I helped Grammy check each cottage refrigerator to make sure it was empty, unplugged, and left open so it doesn't stink in the spring.

I'm sitting on a picnic table when Ronan comes and sits next to me. "Hey," he says.

"Hey," I say, and we sit there quietly for a while. My head fills with thoughts like a tide pool just before high tide.

A question bubbles to the surface, and I turn to Ronan. "You mind if I ask you something?"

He half laughs. "Well, you can *ask* anything."

"The day you hit those kids. The horseshoe crab day. Why did you do it?"

"Being dumb. That's how."

"No, I mean, *why*?"

He looks at me. His eyebrows are all smooshed up. "You know why. They were going to hurt that horseshoe crab."

"But you didn't have to hit them."

"I was mad."

"At them?"

He stares straight ahead. "Why are we *talking* about this?"

"Because I've been thinking about storms. And wind . . . and people." I turn to him, and he's watching me. I blurt out, "Ronan?"

He drops his head. I think he knows I have a tough question coming.

"What is your mom's name?"

He takes a slow breath. "Andrea Gale. *Why?*"

"I was wondering, that's all. You were mad that day at the beach. She wrote you that letter."

He turns to me. "Like I said, why do we have to talk about this?"

I stay quiet and wait, like Esme does for me.

Finally he speaks. "*It's for the best,* she said. I couldn't believe she actually wrote that down, sealed an envelope, and mailed it to me."

"Do you miss her?"

"She's my *mom*."

I swallow hard. Because I understand.

"I had a picture of my mom in this frame next to my bed," I tell him. "And one day I got really mad and smashed it. I didn't mean to. It just . . . *happened*. I mean, I felt mad, but it feels like when we're mad, it's really just throwing a bunch of stuff in a blender, you know? Like sadness and confusion and feeling like nothing's fair. I wonder if you can *just* be angry without all the other stuff. It's like a recipe."

He leans back a bit. "Yeah. I know a lot about anger, but I guess we each have our own recipe for it."

"Maybe anger is like the wind."

"*Anger . . . wind?* What are you talking about?"

"Like, all these things have to happen inside us at the same time and mix together just right, and you get angry. So angry you can't sort through it all. And the same goes for wind. Lots of things that have to happen just right, with the earth moving underneath making it harder for the wind to stay in its patterns. And you really can't *see* wind. You can only see how it moves everything around it. And anger is like that, too."

"You are smart, but you are the biggest dork in the world, you know that, Delsie?" He looks amused with my crazy theories.

I smile. "Thank you." And I think for a moment more. "You know when hurricane winds grow quickly, when they explode, meteorologists call that *rapid intensification*, and I guess it's super hard to predict. But . . . I think I felt that way when I broke the frame."

"Yeah. I feel that way a lot, I guess."

I can tell there's a squall inside he's trying to sort out, too. And then he turns to me. "I think you're right. Wind and anger being alike. You can't stop the wind. But you can *use* it."

"Yeah?" I say.

"You know, I've been thinking about what my dad said. About his temper. I used to get in trouble a lot for fighting and stuff. And I used to say I couldn't help it. But it turns out . . . I *can* stop myself. If I stop to think. Feeling mad doesn't mean I can't control what I *do*. I used to use being angry like it was an excuse. Like it wasn't my fault. But I can stop myself. And it feels good."

"That's good, Ronan. *Really* good."

He nods.

"Grammy says when people hurt, they hurt other people even if they don't mean to," I say. "I bet your mom was caught in a storm herself. I bet she didn't want to hurt you."

"You don't even *know* my mom, Delsie."

"Yeah, but I know *you*. And no one would want to hurt you."

He nods again, and we both stare out at the water.

And my mind skips to Papa Joseph and remembering how we'd always go and check the beach every spring, to see how much damage was done by the fierce nor'easters that pummel the elbow of the Cape. Chatham Beach would look like a completely different place each year. I learned it's the storms that really change us. Not the blue-sky days.

I think about Olive and how her being annoyed and angry all the time must mean that she is really sad deep down.

I think about Michael and how he feels about having to spend summers in the campground. It isn't just the campground that bothers him. It's that he has no say.

And I think how I used to wake up mad and sad earlier this summer. Telling myself how unlucky I was with my grammy in our little neighborhood.

But maybe I was missing something or should have tried to look at it in a different way.

I think I've decided that it's not what you look at that counts, but what you see.

Chapter 47

THE BIG ONE WITH THE LADDER

Ronan shows up at my door in a pair of new running shoes. "Now I'm gonna be a real running machine like you. You better watch out."

"Really?" I say. "You think so?"

"Well, I'm not the runner that you are—*yet*. But I signed up to run in the 5K with you. I know you're doing it for your papa Joseph, and I want to, too."

"Thanks, Ronan. That's really cool," I say. "How about we race to Saucepan Lynn's? I've got a crazy idea I want to talk to her about."

"Of course you do," Ronan says, and with that, we break into a sprint.

It feels good to have Ronan running next to me.

Like they always do, the tides have shifted again.

And the only little voice I hear is Papa Joseph's. He always told me that when you're running a race, it's important to look forward and not back.

• • •

We burst through Saucepan Lynn's door, and Ronan nearly trips on one of the dogs. "Sorry, girl," he apologizes.

"Hey! Don't be running in here like you're on fire!" Saucepan Lynn yells.

"Should a firefighter say something like that?" Ronan asks with a smirk.

"Exactly. I'll throw water on the both of ya." She laughs to herself as she flips the perfect crepe, then slides it onto a plate and points at the ceiling. "I think of you every day, Ronan. With this stain on the ceiling here."

"Sorry about that."

"No sorry necessary. If I'm to be honest, I kind of like it." She leans toward him. "You want another try?"

"Naw, I'm moving on to pancakes."

She shakes her head. "Another one lost to pancakes." Then her head pops up again. "So, RONAN," Saucepan bellows. "I have to tell you. Henry was in here this morning talking about you *again*. I don't know that I have seen Henry Lasko that impressed by a person he's just met—of any age—in a long time."

"Huh?"

"But listen. You really have to give up chasing great whites, okay?"

A guy down at the other end of the counter yells, "This is *that* kid?" Then he takes a good look at Ronan. "Geez, kid. And you dress like a seal. And you're jumping in after sharks?"

Another guy laughs. "Better watch it, Lynn. Don't want to get this one mad."

"I think I can handle him," she says, looking sideways at us.

"I don't know," the man says. "The kid is willing to fight great whites. Not to say that's a smart thing to do! Brave, maybe. Loyal for sure. But . . ." The guy shakes his head. "It's probably the loyalty that gets Henry, though. He loves that. Just think how ticked off he gets when free agents leave the Sox to go somewhere else? Like Jacoby Ellsbury. He's never going to get over that one."

Saucepan Lynn says, "All I know is that Henry says he'd be welcome to work aboard the *Reel*. That tells you something."

Then she turns toward the door and yells, "You better leave something in that bucket, or the next time you'll have a table next to the restrooms."

The guy stops. "*Listen.* I poured my own coffee. Served my own pie."

"And who cooked for you? Did *you* cook it?" She points at us. "Did they cook it? *No.* So don't give me any lip and drop at least a couple of Washingtons in there. You can *afford* a Lincoln. I know how the lobster market is doing."

The guy takes out his wallet and drops in a few bills.

Once the door closes behind the annoyed fisherman, I turn to Ronan. "So . . . um . . . I know it's an honor that Henry wants you on the *Reel*, but can I just suggest you not be a fisherman? You'd throw everything back in the water."

Ronan smiles. "Yeah. I love animals. Actually, I've been studying up on horseshoe crabs. And, hey, I forgot to tell you that yesterday when my dad and I were clamming, I found an *enormous* one—probably about twenty years old. I took her way out into wicked deep water, just in case. Oh . . . and I didn't get into any fights over it." He holds out his fist and we fist bump.

"Positives," I say. "Positives."

"They are so amazing," Ronan continues. "Their blood is blue, *and* it can detect really small amounts of bacteria, so scientists use it to test vaccines."

"Do they kill the crabs to do that?" I ask.

"No, they just take some blood and let the animals go. But I'd like to work on figuring out how to make man-made crab blood so we can leave them alone completely."

"Good idea," I tell him. "It would be so cool if we both became scientists someday . . ."

Saucepan Lynn approaches. "So, you two going to gab all day or order?"

"Well, we actually came to ask a favor," I say. "There's something that needs doing in our neighborhood. Any way we can borrow a fire truck? The big one with the ladder?"

Chapter 48

A GIFT FROM PAPA

It's late, but I'm wide awake thinking about my plans for tomorrow. The box fan roars, but it's too hot to sleep without it. Especially with a kitten cuddled up next to me.

There is a soft knock on my bedroom door. Grammy swings it open. She takes a couple of steps in, and stops to look at my wall of pictures. She smiles when she reads the sign I made: MEMORY SHAKER WALL. Her fingertips caress a photo of Papa Joseph.

"I just love your pictures," she tells me. "I like how you've changed them. I noticed at first you just had pictures of *things* around the Cape. I like the people here *much* better." She tips her head a bit. "What was that about, anyway? All those things you took pictures of?" she asks me.

"Well, I got into taking pictures of things left behind. Like me."

"Oh, *baby*," she says, reaching out for my arm. She's preparing for a Grammy speech, I can tell.

"I know. It was dumb. I took pictures of all these things until I looked up and realized that everyone else on the beach was taking pictures of things they loved, like people and animals, and I decided that I was sick of standing knee-deep in water and complaining that I was drowning."

Grammy laughs long and hard. And she coughs and sputters, too. "Well, you have the wisdom of someone years older if you figured that out all on your own." When she blinks, a tear escapes.

"Grammy," I ask, "what's wrong?"

"Oh, nothing is wrong," she says, sitting on the edge of my bed. "I guess I'm just feeling all blessed, that's all."

I feel like something big is coming.

"I can't stop thinking," she begins, "of the night you got so angry at me and said that you don't have a real family."

I sit up quick. "Oh, Grammy, I didn't really mean—"

"Hush, now. You know I understand the hole that's left behind by not having your momma here. I do. I know it hurts bad. I didn't come up here for apologies. I came up here to give you something." She reaches into her apron and pulls out a small white box. Not a cardboard box but a fancy one you'd get from a jewelry store.

"You bought me jewelry?"

"No, baby. I have something better. My prized possession.

I don't even wear it because I'm afraid I'll lose it cleaning someone's room, but that seems like a silly waste, doesn't it?"

She pulls out a gold chain with a circle hanging from it. I grab it with my hand and see that it's a disc with a gold ship's wheel on it. I turn it over, and it reads:

To my sweet Bridget,
who is my own wheel of fortune.
Much love forever,
Your Joseph.

"From Papa!"

"Oh yes. He said he'd chosen a wheel for me at the jewelry store rather than a necklace with a shell or a boat because of the shape—how it goes round and round and never ends. Like his love for me." She laughs. "That man had a way with words. He could talk a dog off of a meat truck."

I flip it back over and stare at the ship's wheel.

"Like the love in this family. For me and you. And of course, we just adored your mom, too. God, how we loved that girl."

"Do you still love her?"

"I do. She'll always be my baby." She taps me on the nose. "But so will you!"

She reaches around the back of my neck and puts the

necklace on me. "A reminder that you, Delsie girl, may not have your mother here, but you come from a long line of love. And don't you forget it."

"I won't, Grammy."

She kisses my forehead before she goes.

And I feel a part of something special.

My grammy isn't perfect. No one is, and I don't care. You can't order people up like pizzas to have them be exactly as you want.

The people in our neighborhood will always eat in places like Saucepan Lynn's. And I like it that way. Grammy will never go for pedicures or enjoy shopping for pretty dresses. She's probably always going to cut her hair over the sink instead of going to a fancy parlor. But none of that stuff says a thing about her. Not the things that matter. I'm going to stop thinking about the ways I wish Grammy were different and love her for who she is, just as she loves me.

After lying here for a while, thinking of Grammy and Papa Joseph and all of the memories, I get up, go to the picture wall, and peel off one of Grammy. I take the seal frame out of the drawer and tuck her picture inside. When I put it back down, I finally have a picture next to my bed that makes me happy.

Chapter 49

THE SHELTERING TREE

Like the way you can smell a summer rain, you can smell the excitement in our little neighborhood. We're all excited for Olive's big surprise.

Ruby is wearing her new glasses as she pushes open the screen door.

"Hey, those glasses look awesome, Ruby!"

"Delsie! I can *see* everything. But I like the trees the best."

I'm confused. "You could see trees before, right? Trees are huge."

"Yeah, but I didn't know trees had leaves. I thought they had green blotches." She jumps off of her porch. "I just can't stop looking at them now!"

Esme calls her, and she bolts. Watching her run, one

thing is for sure—she isn't clumsy at all. I'm sure it's a relief to see clearly.

Ruby bounces to Olive's and Esme follows. The two of them are in charge of keeping her busy while we prepare the surprise. Getting into the car, Olive seems like a crab that's been caught and dropped in a pail.

When the fire truck arrives, Saucepan Lynn folds her arms as she looks up at the giant pine tree in the middle of our neighborhood. "Well, you weren't kidding when you said it was big, Delsie. Now I understand why a regular ladder wouldn't do."

She looks down at all of the boxes of Christmas lights. "This is a crazy idea, but I gotta say, I like that you and Ronan think big. Now, let's get started," she says, motioning to the other firefighters.

A while later, Ronan and his father arrive. Ronan bursts out of their car. "Hey!" he yells. "We did it! We got the keys!" He holds them up like a trophy.

"Hooray!" I shout, and Henry comes over.

"Welcome to the neighborhood," Henry says, shaking hands with both of them. Gusty asks for the keys and Ronan tosses them to him. Then the two men head over to Ronan's new house.

"Man, that's one megalodon-sized tree!" Ronan says, looking up. "What's it going to take? Ten million lights?"

"Yeah, it'll be visible from space."

Then he grabs my sleeve and says, "C'mon. Let's go look at my new house."

As we climb the steps to the porch, we hear Gusty talking from inside. He uses Ronan's name and Ronan freezes.

"Oh, the fishing life," Gusty says. "Of course I miss it. I miss it every day."

Ronan scrunches his eyebrows and drops his chin a bit. Listening.

"I fell in love with it when I was twelve years old. Even when the catch is bad and the weather is brutal. Even when the work is scarce and the government regulations tie you up. There isn't anything better in the world than being on the ocean . . ."

Ronan's chin drops even more.

"Nope," his dad continues. "There's only one thing on this whole planet that could have made me leave fishing . . . that kid out there. You know, he's the best thing that ever happened to me, Henry. We're gonna fix this place up. I'm going to make it good for him and me."

I smile big, but Ronan's expression isn't like that. Squinting, he smiles without showing any teeth and lowers his jaw. He exhales as he drops his shoulders, like he's just unloaded a heavy weight. He curls forward a bit and turns to look at me. "*Delsie*. Did you *hear* that, Delsie?"

"I did, Ronan."

He bites his lip and then breaks into a big smile and looks up at the sky before straightening his back and taking a giant leap up onto the porch. We step into the house, and the place looks like the destruction after a storm. Along with curtains of cobwebs. We leave footprints in the dust. There's a hole in both the wall and the ceiling, and the wallpaper is curling and brown.

"Hey, I love what you've done with the place." I laugh.

Ronan's voice cracks. "*I* think it's absolutely *perfect*."

"It is, Ronan. It really is."

"Let me show you around," Ronan says, running into the kitchen. He points to a huge puddle on the floor. "We have our own pond. Big enough for a boat." He spins and points at a stove with the oven door hanging off. "And as you can see, it features a stove that will cook if we light the whole thing on fire and cook hot dogs and marshmallows on sticks."

We laugh.

He shows me his room. "My dad let me have the biggest bedroom. And look how the drawers are already in the wall. Isn't that cool?" His face brightens. "Oh! And my dad says that my avó is coming to see the house and meet me. I can't believe it."

We are interrupted by the sound of Saucepan Lynn

hooting and hollering outside, so we run to join her. She gazes up at the tree and folds her arms. "Well," she says, "this tree is completely overdone. Magnificent. Just what I would expect from a couple of crepe flippers."

Even though I didn't actually flip a crepe that day, I know what she means.

The sky has finally grown dark when Henry shakes each firefighter's hand. Grammy hands out lemonade. Saucepan jumps on the back of the truck as it pulls away. "Henry!" she says. "You be sure to come by and let us know how things go here."

"Will do!"

We wave good-bye and then run to our houses to turn the lights off. When Esme's headlights shine up the driveway, we're all standing in the pitch dark.

I squeeze the two extension cords in my hand, ready to connect them and flood the whole place in light.

Esme's sweet, strong voice floats through the neighborhood as she and Olive climb out of the car. I turn and see Henry scoop up Ruby after she runs to him. "Daddy," she says in a loud whisper. "It was so hard not to tell the secret."

And he gives her a squeeze. "I'm proud of you, spitfire."

Olive squints as she tries to see in the dark. "What in Sam Hill are you fools all doing out here in the dark? What is this? A mosquito all-you-can-eat buffet?"

My hands connect the cords, and I feel a buzz of electricity as the lights flood our neighborhood in color. Red and green. Blue and orange.

Olive is wide-eyed, her mouth hanging open just like she's always telling Ruby not to do. "Oh my," she whispers as her head slowly tilts upward and the reflected colors from the bulbs paint her face. "What *is* this?" she asks, but it doesn't sound like sandpapery, you-better-give-me-an-answer-right-away Olive at all.

"This is for you, Olive," I say. "To remind you of your family."

"*And*," Esme adds, "to *remind* you that you'll always have family in each of us."

I can't believe it, but Olive starts to cry. She spins on her foot and scurries toward her house.

I sprint and stand in front of her. "It's okay, Olive . . . stay. Please *stay* with us."

"I feel like a fool," she says. "I'm . . . I'm crying, and I ought to be stronger than that."

"Hey," Ronan says, "I've done plenty of crying this summer and I'm plenty strong."

His expression after he says this makes me laugh—like he's surprised by his own words.

Esme and Grammy go stand on each side of Olive and put their arms around her shoulders.

"See?" I say. "We're all family here."

And as I stand under the glow of the lights with every-one, I know that's true.

I listen to Ruby giggling after Grammy tells her that she looks like a movie star in her new glasses, and memories roll through my mind of Grammy clapping too loud at school concerts. Of her telling me I hung the moon even when I didn't deserve it. Of all the times I did something dumb and she gathered me up in her arms and said, "I've got you, now. Your grammy's got you."

And she did.

There's never been a day when she hasn't been there for me. Making fried bologna and teaching me about game shows. Brushing my tangles out in a way that doesn't hurt. Asking me how I am and wanting the real answer. Rubbing my back while I'm sick and fighting with nurses to stay with me.

And now . . . looking into Grammy's denim-blue eyes, I feel lucky that I never had to weather a storm alone—and that Grammy and Papa Joseph were there to step in when my mother stepped out.

My gaze moves across the faces of my neighbors—and I think how every one of them has helped me in some way this summer. And I realize what I've always known—that family isn't really about blood and having the same last name. It's made by the people who love you. Who worry about you and champion you. Who take one look at you and know when you need a talk over that nourishing tea.

I feel silly for having shouted at the rain, complaining about living under a cloud. Thing is, the sun is always in the sky—it just gets hidden sometimes.

I hear Grammy and Esme and Henry laughing and something deep inside starts small but gets bigger and bigger . . . a feeling.

How lucky I've been.

I have never been abandoned.

I have been loved every day of my life.

Dear Readers,

"It's not what you look at that counts, but what you see."

This is an important facet of *Shouting at the Rain*—this idea that people can look at the same situation and see different things.

I struggled as a kid. In middle school, I looked at my life and felt that, perhaps, I was unlucky. Just like in the book, we shopped at tag sales, had a car that required prayer before starting, lived with walls that were coated in soot from the furnace, had friends who were loyal one day but not the next, and I had parents who could not be available to me.

But in high school, it stunned me when a friend commented on how lucky I was. Seeing my life through her eyes did make my perception tip a bit. And upon further study I discovered that you find what you look for. After looking a little more closely, I realized I did, indeed, have many blessings. Moving forward, I decided to shine a light upon my blessings rather than my struggles.

In *Shouting at the Rain*, I wanted to find a fun way to show how we can all look at the same thing and see different things, and so I created anagrams throughout. An anagram is a word or phrase formed by rearranging all the letters from another word or phrase. (For example, the word *listen* is an anagram of the word *silent*—they have the same letters placed in different orders.)

So each speaking character's name is an anagram that is a hint about the character's personality, life, secret, or a trait they have.

So, for example, when you see the character:

KATRINKA SCHOFIELD (the director of the musical *Annie* at the Cape Playhouse)

I see:

IT'S A HARD KNOCK LIFE

If you'd like to work on solving my anagrams, here is a list of the characters' names. Close to the time of the book's release, check my blog for hints and eventual answers. I'll also provide some extra background about their names.

Here they are:

Delsie McHill

Bridget Maeve McHill

Joseph A. McHill

Brandy Fiester

Tressa Bohlen

Ronan N. Gale

Sherman Gale

Aimee Polloch

Michael Poole

Henry I. Lasko

Esmarelda

Ruby Loren

Olive Tinselly

Katrinka Schofield

Saucepan Lynn

Here is one more anagram from the book:

SHOUTING AT THE RAIN

becomes:

THAT NOURISHING TEA

This book is about how authentic connections improve us and heal us. Being vulnerable—sharing personal things about yourself—is a good thing, because it creates connections by creating trust. However, as Grammy tells us, be careful with whom you're vulnerable. Spend time with people who buoy you and protect you and want the best for you. Who'll be honest with you, but also be kind. Relationships should make you happy, not leave you wondering. Like Delsie, learn to speak up for yourself. You deserve that.

Also, try to see your world with optimism and gratitude. Life isn't easy. You will fail at things, experience disappointments, and get hurt. You *can* handle these things. Stand strong. Face these struggles. Lean on others. But keep optimism and gratitude in your pocket; in tough times, they made me resilient and also helped me become a happy human.

I wish the same for you.

Keep those shoulders strong,

Anna Graham

(A.K.A. Lynda ☺)

ACKNOWLEDGMENTS

I would like to honor the people who care for other people's children, who step in when others step out, including foster parents and the many grandparents and extended family who make sure that children are not left behind. Your mark on the world will be a great one. I can think of no higher calling.

Teachers and librarians: Those of you who take the Ronans of the world under your wing, realizing that their anger is often a mask for frustration, sadness, and heartbreak, I thank you. With love, respect, and high expectations, you save these kids. And that's vital, because if we don't dig deep to help the struggling, angry kids, they will become struggling, angry adults.

I would like to thank my editor, Nancy Paulsen. I will always remember your patience in waiting for me to get this "sauce" done. I know that, with any other editor, these characters could not have become who they are. Thank you.

I LOVE being a Penguin! I am grateful for each and every one of you who helps with all author things! Especially Sara LaFleur, who's always a pleasure to work with. HUGE thanks to Maggie Edkins, who designed this spectacular cover. And to all the other "Penguins" (present and past), including Carmela Iaria, Venessa Carson, Rachel Wease, Andrea Cruise,

Trevor Ingerson, Summer Ogata, Brianna Lockhart, Elyse Marshall, Kaitlin Kneafsey, Alexis Watts, Bridget Hartzler, and Cindy Howle. I never take a single thing you do for me for granted. Ever.

Thanks to my friend and agent, Erin Murphy, and the entire EMLA family. I will always be grateful to Erin for setting me on this incredible journey. One I never thought possible.

A big part of this book is how we can make our own family. Often the people closest to us are not in our lives because of blood ties. So, I'd like to thank:

Susan Rheaume, who was my friend back when we started dating our two guys as fifteen-year-olds and later stood by each other as we each got married. You have always told me that if I need anything, you'll be there in a heartbeat, and you know that's reciprocal. You are caring, loyal, and funny. In fact, you are so many wonderful things, but know that among those, you are loved.

Kathy Martin Benzi, who is a treasure. Of you, I have countless memories of fun times and long laughs. You were one of my early examples of what it means to really support someone. To be a true friend. In college, when I needed someone to listen and help me figure out both my past and my future, you were there. You still are. "Hey, Kath . . . can I ask you something?" :-) You are incredible. Love you tons.

Judy and Fran Miller: When we met thirty years ago, I could've never imagined that one day I'd love you like you're my mom and dad. As a young teacher and mom, you held up a mirror, insisting that I had something special to offer this world. This whole author thing has come as quite a big surprise to me; I know it would not have happened without the two of you.

Both SCBWI and SCBWI New England are a blessing. I have met many cherished friends and mentors through these groups. Being a part of both filled a void I didn't know was there. Forever grateful. Special shout-out to Sally Riley, our RA in New England; you have supported and guided so many of us, always leading with that wonderful heart of yours.

Special love and gratitude to Jenny Bagdigian, Liz Goulet Dubois, Cameron Rosenblum, and Julie True Kingsley for being early readers, steadfast supporters, and darn good friends. Ronan would never call you "sandwich friends" or hammerhead sharks.

When Esme first introduced herself to me, I recognized the wisdom and hearts of Janet Bates and Dr. LaQuita Outlaw. You two helped me create Esme. Thank you for this; I love her.

More love and gratitude for these creative friends who have inspired and supported me: Patricia Reilly Giff, Leslie Connor, Katherine Applegate, Laurie Smith Murphy, Jennifer Thermes, Erin Dionne, Kat Yeh, Jeanne Zulick Ferruolo, Elly Swartz, Hayley Barrett, Kristen Wixted, Brook Gideon, Lucia Zimmitti, Kate Lynch, Linda Crotta Brennan, Hayley Barrett, Audrey Dubois, Pam Vaughan, Mary Pierce, Carlyn Beccia, Kristine Asselin, Tony Abbott, Jane Yolen, Heidi Stemple, Kimberly Brubaker Bradley, Nora Laley Hansen, and Jane Bowditch Holtz.

Thanks to the Cape Playhouse in Dennis, Massachusetts—especially Michelle Kazanowski for her generosity with tours and interviews and for letting me attend acting and improv lessons.

Thanks to Brian Basler, who helped with some Cape inspiration. And thanks to the Red Cottage, Jack's Outback, and Grumpy's, which all helped inspire Saucepan Lynn's.

Big thanks to the children and teachers of Biddeford Intermediate School in Maine who inspired me to continue writing this book. You are creative, smart, special, and appreciated.

And now for my "DNA family" . . .

My mum passed away in 2004 and I think of her every day. When we lose our moms, we are never the same. But things were never easy with us. She had battles that I didn't understand as a kid. But I fiercely loved her. I wish we could sit down over tea and talk about the things that have happened—including the Red Sox winning the World Series! Some of the things that I am most proud of exist because I am Rere's daughter.

I'm blessed to have as siblings Karen, Ricky, Johnny, and Michael. And I am blessed many times over in all of my spectacular nieces and nephews—and now their spectacular children as well. (Hi, Emma, Alex, Zachary, Alora, and Maya!) Much, much love to each of you.

Much love to Mum's cherished ones—the Smith, Martin, Steeves, Gilligan, and Pomeroy families.

And for my in-laws, John and Carol Hunt: I met you when I was fifteen years old and you took me in and cared for me. After thirty-five-plus years you still do. I am so grateful to have married into your family. And thanks for giving me the very best gift I have ever had: your son.

Greg: When I wrote about Papa Joseph and his strong shoulders, I was writing about you. You are loyal and kind. You stand strong for your family. We all know that we can depend on you no matter what. The millions of sweet day-to-day things that you do for each of us are never lost on me. I've done some great things in my life thus far, but none better than marrying you.

Kim and Kyle: There isn't anyone on earth who I look forward to seeing more or who makes me laugh the way the two of you do. I treasure the memories of raising you and marvel at the adults that you have become—your caring and intellect, your work ethics and senses of humor, your curiosity and drive to leave your own positive marks on the world all make me proud. And thanks, Kim, for bringing Dave into our family; he is extraordinary. Love you all infinity times around Pluto. Again.